Luis Carrasco lives and writes in Gloucestershire. His debut novel, El Hacho, was published by époque press in 2018. Ghosts of Spring is his second novel.

Luis Carrasco

Ghosts of Spring

Q é

époque press

Published by époque press in 2022
www.epoquepress.com

Typeset in Bell MT Std/Italic & Dante MT Std/Italic
Typesetting & cover design by **Ten Storeys**®

Printed and bound in Great Britain by Clays Ltd,
Elcograf S.p.A.

British Library Cataloguing-in-Publication Data
A catalogue record for this book is available from
the British Library

ISBN 978-1-8380592-0-0 (Paperback edition)

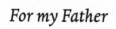

For my Father

Ghosts of Spring

One

SHE carried all her possessions in a single bag save for an old army sleeping sack which she would roll and let hang from the bag to bounce against the backs of her knees when she walked.

Her coat had a fur hood and her boots were good and when she slept she removed them and double knotted them to a hoop sewn into the bag and used the bag as a pillow to prevent it from being stolen in the night. Her feet were always cold in the sack but she refused to sleep with her boots on.

There was a name, crudely tattooed on the inside of her wrist and a bracelet she dared not wear hidden in a screw of tissue deep inside the pocket of her coat. When she lurched from sleep in the night she would pat the bulge in the pocket to reassure herself it was still there. In the bag was a nub of lipstick, a coil of toothpaste and a child's toothbrush decorated with cartoon characters and topped with splayed, yellow bristles.

Her only drink was tea and when she woke in a doorway

to find a hot coffee that she could not drink she always felt the pity of regret. She knew it was a kindness gone to waste in a world with only so much kindness to go around.

Two

SHE touches the inside of her coat and rolls to shift the weight to her other arm and then brings her knees to her chest in the sack. Through the soft bristles of the hood she can see the fabric of night lifting to a fresher blue and soon she hears the gently rising click of heels on the paving slabs. It's a woman's step, short and neat and it taps away in the dark and tempts her back to sleep but then it's lost amid the sounds of other people treading their way to work.

The bark of air brakes from a slowing bus forces her up and she sits in the bag and draws back the hood to let in the day and then straightens her hair with her fingers and pulls it all back and fixes it with a band from her wrist. She sits and shivers and watches her breath roll and knows that the temperature is dropping. She watches them pass wearing heavy-knit scarves and new winter coats and when she opens up her bag to make inventory on her winter wardrobe, she knows she doesn't have enough.

She reaches into the bag for her boots, unties the knot and then pulls them out. She slips her feet from the sack, slides them into the cold leather and laces them up.

She rolls the sack and stands on stiff knees and stares at the spire of the cathedral reaching above the buildings, washed in a corn-coloured light. It flares and dulls as clouds drift across the beam of a low, inchoate sun. Before she leaves she collects the cardboard mat from the doorway and carries it beneath her arm until she reaches the alleyway that runs north from Eastgate. She makes a quick check behind her and walks silently through the alley until she reaches the bracket of pipes where she stashes the mat. It's a good, dry spot and feels like her own private piece of real estate. The previous mat lasted there a month.

She walks back up through Eastgate until it merges into the arcade and then slips amongst the crowd to make a casual tour of the charity shops until she sees the bags piled up against the doorway of the dog rescue shop. Even dogs get rescued, she thinks.

She slides her bag from her shoulders and carefully unties the plastic sacks in the doorway to prevent them from ripping and starts to sort through the clothes and books and board games until she finds something she can use. Everyone that passes her can see what she is and can see what she is doing but she knows they'll never challenge her. She might think this is because they understand that she is as deserving of charity as anybody else and by helping herself to the things that other people happily discard she is just solving the problem directly, but she knows this is not the case. They won't challenge her because they pretend they cannot see her at all.

She selects a few jumpers and some leggings, which are all at least a size too big and then a single blue glove that feels as soft as cashmere. She holds it to her cheek and allows herself a slight purr and quickly looks to find its partner, dipping and weaving through the contents and when she can't find it she opens another bag and then another. She is about to open the final bag when she hears a metallic cascade behind her and standing there is a man holding a plastic flask and a bunch of keys.

Sorry, she says, but doesn't get up and returns her attention to the bag. She wants the other glove.

Don't worry about it.

You want to open your shop.

It's ok. I'm early.

Why would somebody donate one glove?

Happens all the time. Most people aren't really donating, as such, they're just clearing out their drawers. We get a ton of odd socks.

She sifts through the bag but can't find the cashmere glove so she settles for a fingerless pair that aren't as soft but are matching. She starts to refasten the bags.

Don't worry about it, he says. I've got to untie them anyway. Did you get what you need?

She stands to let him pass. I think so, she says. Thanks for not being a cunt.

He bursts into a laugh and lifts a key to the lock.

She walks back through the arcade, stuffing the new clothes into her bag as she walks. She pulls on the gloves and still she thinks of the cashmere and how there might be nothing more useless in this world than a single glove. As she approaches the coffee shop she takes the change from her jeans pocket and counts it in her palm. She walks through the door and the warmth from the overhead heater is the first thing she feels.

She is the only happy person in the queue and this always causes her a smile. The other people hop impatiently from foot to foot and strain their necks to monitor the progress at the counter and check their phones for time and distraction and shape their faces sourly because they are already late to be warm at another place.

She orders her tea and places the change in the girl's hand and waits for it be counted. They ask for a name to write on the side of the cup and she gives a different one every day. Nobody ever notices. Sometimes she forgets which name she has used when the tea arrives. Today she is Skye.

She fills the cup with milk and sugar and tightens the lid and hesitates briefly before leaving, knowing she could stay indoors and drink her tea in the warmth but she also knows she needs to find her spot. She slips to the toilet to brush her teeth and then she's out, pausing in the doorway to feel the final warm push of air on her face.

Three

THERE is mathematical rationale to choosing a good spot and the same formulae is being applied throughout the square. She requires a good footfall of people but not in a place so obvious that she runs the risk of being moved on. She needs to be out of the wind but not hidden in a corner.

Her favourite places in the square are already taken, some by familiar faces, others by shapes she doesn't recognise. To all she has assigned a name, partly to distinguish them but mostly from boredom. Today she can see Tiger-Beard, Shouts-A-Lot, and her favourite, Lives-In-A-Tent, all occupying the premier ground but she is glad to notice the edge of the square between the taxi rank and bike rack unoccupied. There is protection from the wind by the low wall that runs around the grass and it's close enough to the outdoor café, which normally means a gift of food if not money.

She lays down her bag and pulls out one of her new jumpers, folds it neatly into a square, sits on it and crosses her legs. Then she takes out a piece of cardboard the size of a restaurant menu, reviews the wording and straightens out the bent edges where it has weathered and curled. She places it face down on the floor and drinks her tea.

The early promise of sunshine has been betrayed by a pearl grey sky, changeless in colour and weight and spread above the tall horizons of the square. It's still and unthreatening now, but from somewhere deep within it whispers the menace of much colder days to come. She cradles the tea to wrest a little more warmth and then drinks another gulp before flicking the remaining beads of brown liquid onto the floor. She places the empty cup before her, turns over the sign and goes to work.

She never asks openly for money. She still cannot bring herself to do it. She relies upon the sign and a personal aspect designed to elicit sympathy but not intimidate or pressurise. She is too ashamed to meet the eyes of people directly and too proud to stare defeated at the floor, so for hours she sits and looks meditatively ahead or finds some distraction, like a clutter of pigeons tripping around the square for scraps, or counting the cracks in the slabs.

Whenever somebody bends to the cup she makes a point of finding their eyes and thanking them. Suni once told her that it's not the change in people's pockets you are asking them to relinquish but the belief that they are any different to you. Persuade them to believe the two of you are separated by circumstance and not design and that perhaps, by a few unfortunate turns, they could find themselves in a similar plight. Never drink, never smoke and don't demand anything. Charity has its own reward for people, Suni says. It is fuelled by appreciation not expectation. She wonders how Suni can know this as she has never seen her sit for money on the street.

An old man at the outdoor café has been watching her since she arrived and now he stands and fixes his hat and comes towards her. He hands her a flapjack with an unbroken wrapper and then pulls an old banana from his coat pocket and holds it for her to take. The brown spots run from his hand onto the skin of the fruit.

It's a bit ripe, he says.

That's ok, she says and snaps back the neck. Thanks.

How old are you lovely?

She catches his eye and a pulse of suspicion fires inside her. Why?

I've a granddaughter doesn't look no older than you.

Her hair is blowing into her mouth as she eats. Well, she says, hooking it free. Look after her then.

She doesn't want to hang around with an old one like me anymore, he says, but his liquid blue eyes are staring past her to the memory of a little girl that once couldn't wait to play at her grandfather's knee.

She'll be back. Thanks for the food.

That's my pleasure, he says and zips his collar against the chill wind and wanders away.

By four o'clock the wind is chasing litter and school kids around the square and she is bored and numb from sitting. A gang of boys upend the cup as they gallop past her spot but she hasn't the energy to threaten them. She collects the change from the floor and counts past a tenner and stands and stashes the money in her jeans and stuffs the empty cup and jumper in her bag.

With the dusk wrapping coldly around her she walks out of the arcade and finds a café where she buys a tea and steals a sandwich. She moves on through the twilight and stops at a bench tucked into a niche in the wall of an old church, shielded from the road by a bank of old, red phone booths with heavy red doors and dried vomit caked upon the windows.

Along the main road the streetlamps flicker to life. She sits and eats her sandwich and sips at her tea and remembers the flapjack and then the old man and wonders if he is eating alone and where he might be.

She chews and drinks and soon her chin falls to her breast and she sleeps for a while until a squelch of tyres lifts her gaze to a silver van pulling off the main road onto the side street. It passes her and then stops beneath the amber sphere of light blooming from a lamp on the corner. She presses her back against the bench, draws up her legs and watches a man emerge and step out from the shadow and light a cigarette. He takes three quick hits and then flicks it to the floor. He slides back the door on the side of the van and looks up along the street and makes a motion with his hand.

Stiletto heels and the black silhouette of legs scissor out into the light carrying girls that button their coats and spark cigarettes of their own as they drift in small, arm-linked cliques in different directions away from the van. The points of their heels nip at the pavement as they pass her and none of them speak and none of them can see her melded invisibly into the hard iron of the bench and as they lift their hands to smoke, the blush of scarlet light gilds the delicate lines of their painted, determined faces.

Four

A CROWD is forming in the alley when she turns the corner which makes her stop and think about moving on but the hollow bowl of hunger in her stomach urges her forward. The light is fading over the city and almost lost completely in the cobbled tunnel of bins and scabrous render, where hastily scribbled tags bleed together and years of water dripping through the fractured gutters have formed against the walls in green and black rags of kelp.

The wind is tossing needles of cold rain horizontally through the space and the crowd turn their backs to it and trap their hands between their armpits and winch up their spines. Faces marked with the blue of cold and the red of drink flicker smiles as she approaches and one of them, The Bard, standing with an old Spanish guitar roped around his neck, drains a can of cider and throws it to the floor and pulls another from his pocket. He cracks it open and hands it to her. She nods and drinks and hands it back.

Is it not time yet? She asks.

Not yet, he says, looking to his wrist where a watch

once was. They're not even closed yet.

She sniffs and takes another sip from the can. Then she sees the ragged form of a man edge around the group towards her. His arm is held in a dirty sling with bloated, blood-streaked fingers pointing from the mouth of a cast.

What's your name then? He barks, but he's not angry. He just doesn't know a better way to ask.

I know yours, she says.

What?

Broken-Wing. I've seen you in the square mate. When are you gonna get that fucking cast off? You've been walking round with it since the summer.

I know, he says, and splays his feet to find some stability. I keep falling on it, and then I had to go to the hospital and then they said I had to come back, but I don't know when to go, so I just turn up and they tell me I can't come in.

Yeah, cos you need an appointment, says another girl from beneath her hood. They're not just gonna let you in.

I know, he laughs, and the lacquered black stumps of his teeth somehow seem to shine in the faltering light. Give us a sip of that can.

I don't think so, says The Bard and he steps back against the wall causing the guitar across his back to clang tunelessly as it connects.

The bolt on the inside of the heavy metal door echoes the same sound and the door opens and the light pours out. A man with a tray full of sandwiches emerges and places it onto one of the big plastic bins.

They cluster around the tray and lift and pocket the sandwiches quickly but without any selfish intent. Nobody takes any more than their share and when the tray is

empty and the door bolted back into place they walk as
one body through the alley into the better light to review
the take and trade to meet their tastes. When the exchange
has ended the only sound of despair is from a boy with a
wet cigarette behind his ear, his life accrued in plastic bags
at his feet and three prawn sandwiches in his arms that
nobody wants.

I'll swap all three for one of anything else, he pleads
and pulls at the elbows of those beginning to drift away.
They twist themselves free from his feeble grasp and are
swallowed by the shadows.

He turns back to the girl with wind watered eyes.

Come on, he sniffs. I'm starving.

Here, says The Bard, and hands him a baguette.

The kid mutters a thanks and turns the package slowly
in his hand and tilts it to find some light from a distant
lamp so he can read the label.

Chicken, he says and when he looks back up a glimmer
of hope has found its way back to his slender face.

I like chicken.

He stuffs the sandwich into one of his bags and collects
the others from the floor.

Do you want all of them? He asks.

Prawn? Snorts The Bard. I don't want any of them. No-
one does, that's why there's so many of them left at the end
of the day.

What should I do with them?

How the fuck should I know?

The Bard is already walking and the girl falls into his
step. The rain is coming heavier now and it pops against
the wood of his guitar. They enter the square and settle

into the deep recess of a doorway. The girl unwraps a sandwich and picks at it with shivering fingers. He finds a towel from his bag and wipes the rain from his guitar and then lays it down upon the towel with gentle, parental care. He opens another can and sips and stares at the blisters of puddles lying in the square, their glassy skins wrinkled by the prowling fingers of wind.

Where are you sleeping? She asks.

Not sure. My mate lets me use his sofa but only if his missus isn't there. You?

She glances around. Here, probably.

He passes her the can. Do you not use the shelter?

She drinks and hands it back and burps. You have to be on the list.

It's not that hard to get on the list.

I know. I can't be arsed with it.

Warmer than here though, he says and blows through his hands.

It's all the fucking rules though, she says. It's all, in by this time, out by that time, no this, no that. If I'd have wanted to hear all that every night I would've stayed at home.

Where was that?

What?

Home.

Doesn't matter, not round here.

And you can't go back?

I don't want to. He'll still be there.

Who?

Are you the police now? Why do you care?

Alright, he says.

Sorry, she says and pulls her arms inside her coat sleeves and wraps them around her ribs. Can I ask you something?

Go ahead.

Do you only know Beatles songs?

Eh?

I only ever hear you sing Beatles songs.

He looks down tenderly at his guitar. I can play anything, he says, and then reaches to it and slides his fingers up the neck. I was in a band once. A proper band.

Was it the Beatles?

Fuck off.

She laughs and rocks against him and leans there until he admits a smile.

He pulls back a string with a long fingernail and lets it go and the sound tolls out through the square and disappears into the blackened sky like a fleeing bird.

Everybody knows the Beatles, he says quietly. They're worth forty quid a day to me.

Well do us all a favour and change it up, she says. It's boring the shit out of me.

As she shifts her weight on the cold, brick floor she feels a wet heat in her groin and grinds her teeth and sighs and pulls her arms free from the coat and begins to collect her things. She stands and lifts the bag to her shoulder and meets the hopeful face of The Bard.

I've got to go and sort something out, she says. Hope you can get out of this shit tonight.

I'll see you around, he murmurs, his eyes drowned in resignation as he watches her slip into the runnel of the square.

She twists her head into the wind and marches taut-legged around the clots of people making their passage home and dodges past men in suits handling fists of keys and pulling grills across the empty faces of jewellery shops. She rounds the corner and bores towards the bright, yellow font of the McDonalds letters. She is almost running through the entrance and doesn't care who sees her stampede on through the toilet door and fall into the cubicle and lock it fast behind her.

She gathers her breath as she sits on the toilet seat and loosens her jeans and parts her thighs. She reaches down into her pants and lifts out the puck of blood-soaked paper and cups it in her palm and then toes the metal pedal of the waste bin and slaps it into the can.

She brings the back of her hand to her head and then pinches some fresh paper from the plastic dispenser and wipes around her pubis and kicks open the can. Then she collects another ball of tissue, inserts it carefully into place and stands and buttons her jeans.

By the time she collects her mat from the alley and returns to the doorstep, The Bard has gone. As she arranges the mat and unties her sleeping sack she feels a low, empty wave of loneliness that sits with her for much longer than she would normally allow.

Five

A SMALL child, tightly balled in wool stands sentinel before her as she flutters open her eyes and draws back the hood. She wriggles herself up against the door and yawns and wipes some crust from the cracked edge of her lips and still the child hasn't moved. The glossy red shine of her nose and her dark unblinking eyes are all you can tell of the infant hidden beneath the wraps of scarf and hat and thick purple tights.

Hello, she says and the child's eyes widen in wonder.

A woman crashes into the frame and stoops to collect the child's mittened hand and pulls her onto her toes and away with a soft rebuke and an apology to the girl on the mat.

It's ok, she says, I've woken to worse, but they're gone and the view to the square is open to where early shoppers are scudding purposefully from place to place. She unzips the sack and the cold takes her breath so she wraps herself back up and shuffles forward onto the edge of the step. There she lifts her gaze to a hard sapphire sky scored by the white chalk lines of high-flying jets.

She huddles in the sack and watches and waits in the hope that someone will bring her a tea but soon the hunger moans within her. The growing discomfort in her lap reminds her that she must replace the pad so she opens her bag and unties her boots and pulls out the knitted red jumper. From this point on she will be wearing everything she owns. She puts it on and throws her swollen arms through the coat sleeves and ties the sleeping sack to the bag and when she kneels to lace her boots and collect the mat, she notices that someone has left a pound coin on the edge of the step.

She adds it to the change in her pocket and finds she has enough for breakfast without sitting for it on the street. She mouths a thanks across the square to the map of people shuffling barrel-backed against the cold in a honest token of hope that it might find its way to her anonymous donor.

She moves out from the doorway into glacial air and when she walks between the buildings into the shards of sunlight she feels no warmth from it. She orders her tea and a hot breakfast sandwich from the café and uses the toilet to change the tissue in her jeans. She steps back out into the hard light and pecks her lips at the plastic flute of the cup while she looks for a spot in the square to set up for the day. Much of the space is already taken though and soon a weary sense of dejection falls over her.

Christmas is coming, she thinks and knows this should loosen the hearts of people in her favour but she cannot find the will to sit and do it. A voice inside her says you'll starve, but it isn't strong enough to turn her apathy. She finishes her breakfast and slides the mat behind a post box and walks the parquet bricks of Westgate until she comes to the cathedral.

She walks to a stone block and sits. A man works nearby, clearing the flower beds of their winter waste and behind him, another rakes flat the soft brown earth to take the spring planting when the soil has warmed. An old couple in matching beige raincoats, blade thin and bent at the waists, steady each other as they slowly circle the cathedral and point to places they have corresponded from the guidebook he holds against his chest.

She has never been to the cathedral before. The high peak of its nave can be glimpsed from all points of the city, but she has never seen it whole and now she wonders why. An immense bastion of dun coloured stone, with filigrees of crinkled stonework, gaping black mouths of arched windows and long thin towers sprouting from the ramparts into the arc of the low sun and shining like polished bone. It stands before her like an accusation of something she doesn't yet understand. She blinks and draws a thin, powdery breath.

Soon she is tired but doesn't know what to do. The aggregation of aches in her joints from sleeping on hard stone urges her to find something softer to rest upon but no place where she can do this comes to mind so she shifts off the block, collects her bag and walks out from the cathedral grounds heading south into the sun.

The approach of Christmas is conditioning the mood of the streets with shop fronts striving to deliver the vision of a perfect day. Cotton wool snow drifts and children's jumpers for adults, to be worn once and then bagged for the charity shop. People stop abruptly before her, forcing her around them as they stare into the displays hoping they will find the thing that will enable them to tick one more name off that list.

A smart young couple, with armfuls of branded bags step across her to close in on the feast being promoted from the delicatessen. Pyramids of sweets and meat and potatoes and goblets of purple wine. She swerves to avoid them as best she can but catches the man's arm with her rucksack, making him drop his bags. When he turns to see her, his face is apologising before he gets the words out. She laughs and walks on.

The boardwalks of the docks are bouncing with shoppers, stepping lively beneath the tall sides of the old bonded warehouses with their renovated Victorian ensign. After weeks of rain there is a clean, antiseptic quality to the light which angles from the water's gentle chop in timid flickers of gold. She walks with purpose, threading through the crowd like it's a game, curling her body around dogs and pushchairs and teenagers squinting into their phones.

Past the docks the landscape flattens and the streets are a monotony of red brick and corner shops with exotic Polish signs, she cannot pronounce. She enters one and spends the last of her money on a pasty, stuffs it into her pocket next to the bracelet and continues her trek.

At a park on the suburban outskirts of the city she finally stops and sits and eats, breaking small, greasy flakes off the pasty to make it last and when she has finished she waits for the park to clear before dodging into a grove of shrubs to replace the pad. The blood hasn't soaked it through and she feels a relief at knowing its coming to an end.

The day is slipping away from her and she thinks about the journey back to the square and then thinks about sleeping in the park. She dismisses it and makes to stand and leave but then she stops.

Why not? she says and her voice catches brokenly and she imagines she hasn't spoken more than twenty words since she awoke to the sight of the little girl in the doorway. She coughs her throat clear.

It's better here than the square, she reasons. This is a decent neighbourhood. Grass is softer than concrete. Why do you feel safer in the company of dangerous strangers than alone with the trees and birds?

She runs her hand across the carpet of cold grass and wipes the moisture across her jeans and looks around into the thinning light. To her left the falling sun has towed a thick mantle of cloud in its wake, scalding its rim in scarlet as it dips and disappears. Before her the city throws its artificial glow against the dark belly of the cloud and orders her to return.

Six

SWAYING now on leaden thighs she passes back into the square and looks for her mat behind the post box where she left it. It's gone, and she casts a venomous glare around her to see if she might find its new owner. In the doorway she can see the encampment of Lives-In-A-Tent, zippered in for the night and has no way of knowing if he took it.

I should have stashed it properly, she thinks and leans her face into the cold metal of the post box and wonders why the square is so quiet on the Saturday night before Christmas.

She stands and shifts her weight between her feet and wants to be still but can't until she finds a place to sleep. The air feels soft and soon the snow begins to twirl through the white arc of the lamps that ring the square. It floats in thin, weightless flakes, small and grey in the low wattage light of the lamps like ash descending from a fire burning somewhere beyond the perimeter of the city. She slides off a glove and lets a flake settle on the back of her hand and watches it slowly dissolve.

The night has a soft, soporific quality she knows is enticing and dangerous. She could stay and become seduced by its charm and then find herself without cover if the snow starts to come with any weight. She also knows she is without a mat for the night and a slender panic pushes through her stomach so she prises herself away from the box and walks towards the arcade, grunting as her heavy legs are forced back into motion.

The arcade is busy with late shoppers forced to make their rounds after work and girls in tight white dresses high stepping in their heels and rubbing the cold from their bare arms as they trot between the pubs. An older man she knows only as Smiles-With-His-Eyes is crouching with a girl she doesn't recognise on the wide steps of the bank. He calls her to them and then takes the time to fuss over her with a kindness not found in the relatives she once knew and asks her where she is sleeping.

The other girl is sitting in her sack and has a clean, pretty face and is sucking at a roll-up as thin as a toothpick. She shouts at the groups of boys rolling through the arcade, begging them for money and drink without any fear or misgiving and betters them in banter when they stop.

Where are you going now? The sitting girl asks, picking tobacco from her lip.

Dunno. Probably just walk a bit more. You?

Just this. Maybe one of these twats will throw us a note cos they want to be a big man in front of their mates. Have you got any fags?

No.

Don't start, says Smiles, pulling a butt from the padded depths of his clothing. And find somewhere warm, it's fucking snowing look.

I know, she says and hoists her bag across her back and grips his forearm as she passes him. See you in a bit.

Take care babe, the sitting girl shouts behind her.

The girl smiles and walks through the arcade with a face that's searching for something. Then she finds it. Tangles-With-Boys, she laughs and is still smiling when she enters the darkened warren of Barton.

In the grave light of the terraced streets, girls in short-cropped fur and long boots step from the shadows to slowing cars and bend from the waist to rest their elbows on the window frames of the ones that stop. The cars throw poles of yellow light through the snow and the engines turn lightly while terms are discussed. A fracas erupts as the girl passes by, and she pulls her hood across her face and quickens her pace to avoid it.

She turns into a side street and stops at a door and takes her hand from the glove and blows hot breath into her fist. She taps at the wood and waits. She taps again and looks up to the windows on the first floor, her breath glittering in white crystals above her. The house is dark and dormant and she taps again, with ebbing conviction and pulls up her hood and shifts her bag evenly across her shoulders and leaves.

She walks to the bench by the phone box, slides her bag underneath it and huddles into the corner of the seat. She waits and thinks of food and wonders where the best place will be in the square in the morning and is glad for the snow as it spurs people's pity but then realises it's a Sunday and swears and spits onto the pavement.

She sits and watches cars drawing black lines through

the settling white dust on the main road. She blows the flakes from her coat and her eyes become heavy and she wants to stretch out her legs and sleep.

A silver van trawls past with the bodies inside shaded by the tint of the windows. She grabs her pack and follows the van up the street and watches it stop and the girls alight and break into factions. As two of them come back in her direction she steps unseen into an alleyway to let them pass and then falls in behind them, skipping quickly through the yellow cones of light under the streetlamps and then slowing in the pockets of shadow between them.

The two girls enter a house and she waits and counts for a minute and then creeps to the door and raps at the scaly paint work.

Suni's face emerges into the strip of light and her face is tense until the girl pulls back her hood and then she smiles and the white of Suni's teeth is matched by a bright spark at the edge of her black eyes.

Hey chick, she says. What's up?

Nothing. Just seeing if you were here.

We just got back. You want a tea?

Fucking love one, says the girl.

Suni palms the door open and turns and walks through the hallway on stockinged feet. Go straight up, she says behind her. I'll be up in a minute. Don't mind Cam, she's just using my shower.

The girl quietly presses the door back into the lock and stands on the mat and looks at her boots and breathes the easy, warm air of the house. Her boots are rimed with snow, so she slides off her bag and kneels to untie them and then has to sit to wrestle them off her feet. She opens the door to bang them free of snow and pairs them on the mat and pulls up her socks and carries the pack up the stairs on a cloud of soft, downy carpet.

In Suni's room she rests her hand on the radiator top and the heat from the metal burns her numb fingers like an open flame. The door to the bathroom is open and water is pounding from the shower. A gauzy mist drifts through the room bringing with it the sweet, exotic lines of citrus fruit. She is light-headed from the sudden change in temperature, grabs at the zip of her coat and leans free from it. She pulls the red jumper over her head and throws it onto the bag, then lifts a pile of magazines from a tub chair, places them onto the bed and collapses into the chair and moans at the softness.

Suni carries three mugs through the door and spits a mouthful of crisp packets onto the bed. She places the mugs on the dresser and some liquid slops over the rim. Shit, she says and wipes the dresser and the bottom of the mugs with a sock and then throws it onto a wicker basket already overrun with clothes.

The girl looks at the heap and then around the room at the towers of plates and glasses and the lights tumbling unevenly from the shelves.

You are a proper messy bitch.

I know.

I've slept in alleyways cleaner than this.

Well you can go back there then.

The girl is hot under her layers and dots of moisture are beginning to form on her lip. She sits forwards to peel free another jumper and blows with the effort.

Suni is still staring at her. Did you eat today, babe?

What?

It's ok to be hungry when you come here.

The girl nods.

Just because you eat here sometimes, it doesn't mean that I only think you come here for the food.

I know you don't.

Good. Suni throws two packets onto her lap. Start with these and we'll get you some toast.

Alright.

I mean it though, you don't have to feel...

Alright, Suni, for fucks sake. To be honest I could be this hungry for another couple of days and it wouldn't really bother me. Crisps are fine.

Suni smiles and reaches for her mug. She lies back against the headboard, flinches and shifts her weight to her elbow. She gently tilts the mug to her mouth and whistles cool air at the rim and watches the girl obliquely as she ploughs through the crisps. She rubs the tired from her eyes and looks at the greasy sludge of mascara lifted upon the ball of her thumb and then drives a critical survey down the length of her body.

I need to get this stink off me, she says, placing the mug on the floor by the bed.

Cam! She shouts.

The churn of water from the bathroom slows to a thick drip and then the sound of a door sliding on a rail. Suni levers herself onto her feet and arches her back to find the zip at the top of her skirt and above her the pipes in the attic gong as the air becomes locked in a joint.

Camila steps from the bathroom wrapped in a blue towel with the skin scrubbed pinkly on her cheeks and her hair wrapped up high in another towel. She pads through the room carrying a ball of clothes before her and nods to the girl on the chair.

I made you a coffee, Suni says as she moves to let her pass.

I'll come and get it.

It'll be cold.

I'll drink it cold then. I'm coming back.

Suni eases her hips up out of the skirt and sits on the edge of the bed to roll her stockings in doughnuts down her legs and throws them onto the heap. She stands and skins the tight black top from around her waist up and over her shoulders and then pinches at the clasp of the bra behind her back and punches her shoulders forward to cast it off and stands in her pants and takes a slurp from Camila's coffee on the dresser and turns to the girl.

You want a shower after me?

Sure, says the girl.

As Suni passes from the gloom into the bright light of the bathroom, the girl sees the grill of red lacerations running like a ladder from the backs of Suni's thighs, up around the curve of her rump and on past the caramel bowl of her back to the plane of her neck.

Seven

THEY stand over the girl sleeping in the chair. Drinking tumblers of black wine they study her posture, the knee lifted up across the arm rest and her hand bent sharply at the wrist for the backs of the fingers to form a platform to cushion her chin.

She was out before I even got in the shower, Suni says, her damp hair resting in curved black daggers down the white towelling of her gown

Camilla sips her wine and bends down to the girl's face.

She's dead to it.

I know.

Where does she normally go?

To sleep? On the streets. I don't think she uses the shelter.

Fuck that, Camilla says and bounces onto the bed and pushes the sleeves of her jumper up past her elbows. She refills her glass from a bottle standing on the floor.

You ever do it? She asks.

For a bit, Suni sighs. Not for long

Here?

Oxford.

Why there?

It was all the train fare I had when I left London. Walked into the station and that was the first one leaving. You?

Nope. I literally don't think I could make it through a night.

Suni laughs. You're such a wimp.

I am. I don't care.

The girl flicks unconsciously at some irritation on her nose and twists in the chair and finds another point of comfort and sleeps. Suni lowers herself to the edge of the bed and then shifts her weight painfully and cradles her glass as she stares at the girl.

You know she can't stay here, Camilla says quietly.

Suni heaves a deep and measured breath and releases it in parts. He's not gonna come here tonight, she says.

You don't know that.

When has he ever come here after a shift? He's just dropped us off.

He might in the morning.

He might. I'll get her up early.

I'm not being a bitch Sun. I like her.

I know. I know the rules.

Camilla flexes her legs forward and massages her hand into the soft flesh of her neck. She stares at the girl.

Good looking kid though, she says. If he found her lying here he'd kick right off, but he might want to work her. Does she know what we do?

Suni rolls her eyes. Of course she does.

She's never worked?

Don't think so.

You think she might?

Suni's eyes flare. Leave it Cam. There's no fucking way. The shit they made me do tonight.

She reclines and lays her head into Camilla's lap and fingers her wet hair past her ear.

It's getting desperate up there, says Camilla softly. I want to get us out, not get another one in. But it's winter and it's getting really cold and if we start letting her sleep here, she's gonna keep coming back. I know I would.

Suni presses her face into Camilla's crotch and breathes the chemical flora of the washing powder in her pyjama's and then lies up next to her, tucked into her armpit and stares at the ceiling.

I'll wake her early, she says, and leans to the edge of the bed to place her glass on the floor. Then she rolls back up into Camilla's arms and lets herself drift into dreams that are fractured and senseless and real.

When the girl wakes she is shining in sweat. Cam lies asleep in the bed and mauve light is creeping around the edges of the blinds. She reaches out from the chair and hovers her hand above the radiator, turning it slowly over the rising heat. She stretches her legs and unfurls into a cavernous yawn and stands and walks to the dresser.

Scattered there are make-up pencils and brushes dusty with blusher and discarded face wipes covered with black and grey stains. She reaches forward, gathers a handful of tampons and stuffs them into her bag. Then she lifts up a picture frame with a thick silver edge and stares at the faces of two young children with hazel skin and carefree smiles wearing novelty sunglasses shaped like stars. Suni's sister is younger and is wrapping her arm up and around

Suni's neck to pull her own head into the shot.

She replaces the frame and looks at her own reflection in the mirror. A spot is forming above her eyebrow and she leans forward to find some purchase and pops it onto the mirror. She cleans off the pus with a used wipe and tosses it back onto the dresser. Then she sees the grime under her nails and the chapped white skin on the backs of her hands. She bares her teeth into the mirror, sticks out her tongue and stares deeply into her own eyes and wonders if Suni will still let her shower.

The faint collection of noises from downstairs tells of a kitchen being worked. She slips from the room and treads cautiously down the stairway and into the hall and through the open door of the kitchen she sees Suni standing at the cooker stirring a pot and grooving her head to some tinny music coming from a phone perched on a shelf.

Hey, she says, but not loud enough for her to hear, so she comes up behind her and lays a hand onto the soft fabric of her back.

Suni turns and pulls her in for a hug and the wooden spoon upends from the pot and hurls globes of rice onto the tiled wall behind the cooker.

I'm glad you're up, she says. I didn't want to have to wake you but…you know.

The girl yawns and pulls a chair from beneath a small table and sits.

You want some tea?

Always.

Suni clicks the kettle and returns to the pan. Alright, she says. But you are definitely having some of this.

What is it?

Suni chuckles and pecks her fingers into a ceramic bowl, draws a clutch of powder and dresses the food in the pan. Then she squeezes a thick line of honey into the mixture and scoops up a palmful of raisins and chopped nuts and drops them in and stirs. She collects two bowls from the sink, wipes them with a towel and divides the food between them before placing them on the table. The girl opens her nose above her bowl and the sweet notes of the honey makes the sides of her tongue run with water.

It's hot, Suni says, passing her a spoon.

The girl lifts a wedge of food and blows and eats. It's really fucking good she says, her grateful eyes gleaming. What is it?

Suni smiles. My nan made me this every morning when I was kid. I still can't get it as good as hers.

The girl is spooning huge loads into her mouth.

What's the smell like perfume?

Saffron.

Is there any more?

A little bit, yeah.

As they eat Camilla shuffles into the door frame with puffy eyes and her hair caught up in a knot that has slipped across her head in the night.

Jesus, Suni says. What are you doing up?

I heard you two banging on. Can we have a word?

Let me finish this.

No, now Sun.

It's alright, says the girl, laying her spoon down into the bowl. I'll get my shit together.

Don't stress, Camilla says, unwinding the hostility in her pose. It's not your fault, it's hers. Finish your breakfast, but then you'll have to go cos we're all fucked if this carries on.

The girl picks up her spoon and scrapes it around the bowl. Camilla shakes her head and humps back up the stairs.

Would you really get kicked out, just for me being here?

Suni straightens herself on the chair and pulls at her ear and finds a loop of hair and curls it around her finger. She sits thinking.

I don't know, she says finally. It's not getting kicked out of the house that bothers Cam, it's more like, losing the whole setup. We're not ready yet.

I don't know what that means.

Suni stares gravelly at the table and breathes slowly and the thick white folds of her gown billow on her chest. Then she raises her head and smiles archly at the girl and her eyes have a defiant depth.

I'm gonna tell you, just so you know. Cos I'd have you here for as long as you need to get yourself straight if it was that easy.

It's alright Sun, I wasn't…

It's ok. I'm not ashamed of it. It is what it is.

She looks out through the window and composes herself.

Those girls out there in the streets are rolling the dice every night with what they do. You can believe me cos I've done it. As soon as you climb into that car there's no one behind you if they turn out to be a psycho and the fear never leaves you until you climb back out and for what? Fifty quid and if he wants to be a prick about paying, what are you gonna do?

We work one night a week and don't get me wrong, it's a fucking freak show up there, but we're driven there and back and we get paid every month. Into a bank account mind, and this house comes with it. That's why we don't have a say about who we let in here.

The girl sits and rubs at the dry skin on her hands.

You can ask me about it, Suni says.

The girl shifts on the chair and makes to speak and stops.

It's alright. Ask me.

Is it the guy with the van that owns the house?

Him and others.

Where do they take you?

Some massive, fuck-off place up in the hills. Like a stately home, you know what I mean.

The girl nods. But how can they pay you so much for just one night?

Suni laughs a dark, caustic laugh.

Because we're hot and we're not junkies and we know why we're there. Because they are respectable and rich and they don't have to risk getting girls off the street. But mostly because you'd never get a human being to do what they want us to do for anything less.

Eight

THE warmth of the library is making the windows drip with condensation. The snow bulks on the sills outside and hangs to the undersides of the frame and when the girl swabs the pane and peers through, small pins of light fizz and shiver in the bands of white.

A woman in a silk blouse the colour of the snow and a long red skirt and red ballet pumps floats past her and caresses the pile of books on the desk with her fingers as she passes.

Twenty minutes love.

What?

The woman turns and smiles and her face is pink and kind. Pinned onto her chest is a leaf-patterned brooch that pulls clumsily at the fabric of her blouse and misshapes it and ruins the effect and makes the girl wonder what made her wear it.

Twenty minutes until we close. You can leave the books in the basket at the front though.

I thought you closed at six?

Five on Christmas Eve though lovely. And we're not open again until the third so if you want to take anything out you need to do it now.

She doesn't have a library card nor any fixed address with which to acquire one. She revolves the block of books on the desk so she can read the spines. Only one carries her interest. She has half read it before and wrote an essay on it for her A levels and she smiles at the memory and thinks that if she had another chance she would read it properly and try for a better mark.

She watches the woman disappear into the corridors of high shelving on the far side of the hall and looks up at the counter where the other librarians work and then skims the book from the desk and traps it between her knees. Then she unties the bag leaning against the leg of the desk and pushes the book deep amongst the folds of her sleeping bag. As her hand comes up she feels the plastic of the toothpaste tube. She runs her tongue around her teeth and stands and pulls on her coat and collects the remaining books and walks to the counter to drop them in the basket.

She walks past the double wooden doors of the library entrance and on towards the toilets. Inside she stands the bag on the shelf by the sink and unzips a side pocket and pulls out her toothbrush. Her lipstick topples out with it and she balances it on the shelf.

The tube is there in her hand and is fat and full and she can't remember why she didn't ask Suni if she could have it when she was leaving the house rather than stealing it. She thinks of the book and wonders if she is a criminal.

She brushes her teeth slowly because her gums are tender and sore and when she spits there are tails of blood running through the white patty of spume. You need some fruit, she thinks and swills her mouth and spits and swills until the blood has gone. She replaces the toothpaste and brush into the bag and then pulls off her woollen hat. She rakes at her scalp and finger combs her hair back down, wishing she'd had time to shower before she left Suni's. She lifts up the lipstick and clicks off the cap and slowly twists the golden cylinder until the waxy shard of red emerges.

She lifts her chin to the mirror and leans in to push out her lips and smears an economical band across each lip and then mashes them together. She lifts her fingers up to push the colour into the corners and then dabs her fingertips onto the mirror imprinting two round discs of red. She blows a cheap kiss at herself and leaves.

Outside on the pavement her boots crackle as she walks and although the night is cold and the snow is coming in wide, ragged flakes and standing where it falls, she has a belly-full of food and a new mat to sleep on. She also has some money Suni forced on her when she was leaving the house and knows this will see her fed until the New Year without having to sit for it over Christmas when the streets will be empty of anybody who isn't drinking.

She kicks her feet through the snow and heads towards the arcade. On the road to her right the cars inch forward through the traffic, heaving sulphurous white clouds of exhaust that rise and absorb the red of the lights. She passes across the entrance of the square and to her left, under the scaffolding stacked against the old Woolworths building, lies the hump of a body. She watches as people round the corner and nip under the boards to find some shelter and then recoil as they see the prone figure obstructing their path, step quickly into the street and pass on.

She creeps closer and stares. People drift around the orbit of the body. An old couple holding each other at their elbows and skater kids and shoals of blokes in shirts and jeans and then a woman in a fleece with the blue glare of her phone reflected in her glasses. They all float past the body under the planks the way the snow wends its indifferent path to the ground.

A few more steps bring her closer and now she can see the grimy triangle of the sling folded across his chest and the tufts of his beard caught with snow. He mumbles and hacks with a cough that rolls him onto his side and as he releases the can from the purple fingers sprouting from his cast, it lists onto the ground and drains.

She drops down next to him and the ground is cold and wet beneath her knees.

This fucking guy, she says and pulls him onto his back.

Come on, she says and slides a hand beneath his head. His eyes swivel and he moans an incomprehensible logic of appeal.

Where are you sleeping? She shouts, the words bouncing off the shell of his oblivion. Where are you supposed to be mate?

He drools and laughs and slurs a word that sounds like shelter.

She's up on her calves and trying to lift him but he's boneless and heavy in her arms and she grunts and blows through her nose and lowers him back down.

Shit, she says and stands hip-handed and works out the distance to the shelter. Around her people slow and move on and then a kid with a pea-coat and biker boots detaches from his group and draws next to the girl.

Is he alright?

He's pissed and he needs to be around the corner. I can't leave him here.

Do you know him?

No, but I can't leave him here.

How far does he need to go?

Just down there and round the corner.

Alright. He's gonna need to be on his feet. There's no way you'll carry him.

She turns to him as he as he passes her.

Thanks.

Come on mate, he's saying to the body as he cups it under the armpits and hoists it up, rolling himself underneath the good arm as he gets the man standing. He staggers under the weight and nods to the girl to prop the other side. She hops forward and leans into the ribs to avoid any pressure on the arm and the broken white wing folds down over her.

They stumble and skitter out from beneath the scaffolding and inch up the street. His feet are in contact with the floor but unable to support his weight and his legs drag brokenly behind him as they encourage him to support himself. He leans his face into the girl's and spit bubbles on his lips and his breath is animal and rank.

As they round the corner to the shelter he slumps upon her, forcing her to take the weight on his arm which makes him squeal with pain. He twists in their grip and they drop him to the floor. The kid stands and sucks rapidly at the frosted air.

How much more?

Hang on, she says, and runs towards the lights at the

entrance to the shelter. On the steps stand two big men in matching black coats and laminated lapel badges.

Hey, she says and pauses to gather her breath.

Not tonight love.

What?

We're already jammed.

I'm not looking for a bed mate. I wouldn't stay here if you fucking paid me.

Alright. Calm down.

I think I found one of your lot face down in the snow. He's at the corner. Can you come and sort him out?

What's his name?

The girl smoothers a smile. I don't know.

What's he look like?

She raises her hands to describe him. Somewhere between forty and sixty, stinks of piss and out of his mind. Broken arm.

One of them tilts a glance at the other. Billy, he says. The other one nods.

Ok, she says. Billy. Can you come and help? I can't drag him any further.

Yep. Where is he?

On the corner. Look you can see him.

They step off the porch and follow her to where the kid is standing. Relief covers his face as the big men approach. The girl stands back and watches as one of them bends to the body and says his name and then hoists him onto his back as if he were made of felt. She gawps in admiration and remembers the way her own father would scoop her from the floor as a child and carry her up the stairs across his shoulders and drop her onto her bed for stories.

They cart the body up the street and the kid stands awkwardly in front of her.

Thanks, she says. You didn't have to do that.

His eyes shine. Don't worry about it, he says and pulls up the wide collar of his coat. Are you alright?

Yeah.

Some girls pass and call his name and he reacts and tells them he's coming and to wait for him and then he looks back at the girl and she feels a movement in the pit of her stomach that makes her cross her legs at the ankles.

Happy Christmas, he says.

She nods and watches him turn and skip to catch the girls and lock arms as they march up the street together and become steadily eclipsed by the blizzard.

Nine

IN THE hard hours before dawn she drifts around the upper tiers of sleep. Her body vibrates with the cold and she rolls around in her sack and pushes up against the wall at the end of the alley, clutching at the bulge in the inside pocket of her coat and whimpering with a shattered breath. She's folding and forcing her limbs into a ball to find enough heat and comfort to sleep but the frigid air seeps through her swaddled layers.

Shuddering, she sits up against the wall and rests her head against the rough brick. Above the high sides of the alley, a purple-black rectangle of sky is punctured with the shimmering dots of stars. She shivers and wishes for a new snowfall and the insulating warmth the heavy cloud brings to the city but the sky is high and clear and raw flint winds are screaming past the mouth of the alley.

Christ, she mutters. How can it be this cold? She yawns and slides back down to the floor and rocks there gently, her hands clamped between her thighs. She slips into a messy collage of images, scenes and memories, too formless and quick to be dreams and always she is aware of the hard surface eating at her hips and shoulders and the vein of cold running through her.

Moaning, she wakes and draws a hand up from the sack to slide her hat from her eyes. Above the alley walls she can see the blue of dawn and the stars beginning to pale in the changing light. Fangs of ice cling to the roof tiles above her and they quiver in the wind and threaten to break and fall. Too numb and tired to care she closes her eyes to her fate and wonders if it will be quick and painless.

On the floor ahead of her an empty can of lager gets lifted by a spur of wind and spins and clinks upon the cobbles and mites of snow, prised from the heavy banks on the pavement, skid through the mouth of the alley on the same gusts.

She thinks of her own room in her own house and then wonders if she can still claim them as her own. She remembers her bed, low to the floor but sprung and warm with four pillows and sequined cushions that she would toss to the floor before she climbed in to sleep. A wooden box at the foot of it with extra blankets and a thinner duvet for when the other one made her too hot in the summer. She closes her eyes and sees her college artwork and band posters spread across the walls and smiles at the ones with the folded corners where the pins had come loose which she was never bothered to fix. White shelves of books and a wardrobe full of clean clothes.

She can still claim the memory.

With the cold breath of the alley on her cheeks she opens her eyes and throws her arms from the sleeping sack and digs into her bag to untie her boots from the loop.

After two nights alone there and frozen to the marrow, she wants to leave even though she knows she has no better, warmer place to go.

Tea, she thinks. I could get a tea.

She slides the boots out from the bag and into the sleeping sack and laces them blind and slowly zips the sack apart. The air nips through her coat and quickens her breath so she kicks out her legs and rolls to her feet and grabs at the bag to buckle it shut. She throws her arms through the straps and then collects the sack, unzips it to its base and then curls it around her shoulders for a shawl.

She moves through the alley and out into the street and slumps up the road like some ragged itinerant ascending from the sewers, cloaked and hunchbacked with hungry, sliding eyes.

Under the pale light of the streetlamps the road is a hard pan of milky white ice with a spine of grey snow running up the centre where the tyres don't run. Cars emerge from side streets, their wipers scraping black triangles into their windscreens as they drone past her in small gears. As she approaches the entrance to the square the street lamps die and hum on their stalks and the snow on the pavement turns from white to a purple grey.

The shops in the square are brimming with sale signs and young girls bend behind the windows to change the displays. Some stand outside and suck quickly at cigarettes, flicking them half-smoked into the piles of ice that have been scraped from the doorways and then rap impatiently on the glass to get in to begin their shift.

She crunches a path across the square and into the Starbucks where she stops and stands under the oasis of heat falling from the ceiling, moaning gratefully and wanting to get higher and closer up to it. The automatic door slides open and closed behind her and a man reading a newspaper at a table turns mean lipped at the source of the draft.

She shuffles up to the counter, still wrapped in her sleeping sack and the girl looking up from the coffee machine can't mask her surprise. She has ginger plaits trailing from beneath her cap and a ring of acne around her mouth. Her name badge has Becky stencilled in bold letters.

What can I get you?

A tea and one of these, says the girl stabbing a finger to a pastry in the cabinet.

Large or regular?

Large.

What's the name?

Becky.

She looks down at her badge and then back up.

Becky, she says.

Yep.

Ok then. Milk and sugar is over there, she says, pointing to the stand.

The girl moves to the stand and is beginning to thaw. She lifts a paper square of sugar from the metal box and rips off the corner and pours it into her mouth and crunches on it slowly. More people are stepping through the door and pausing in relief under the heat of the blowers and every time they come, the draft slaps at the neck of the newspaper man who twists his head around accusingly.

Move, you prick, thinks the girl. There's empty tables

all over the place, and in warmer spots too. Then she works on a name and smiles and wonders if she can let him into the club even though he isn't technically on the streets.

Becky shouts 'Becky' and the girl moves back to the counter to collect her tea. She pockets the pastry and plucks the plastic lid from the tea and fills it with milk and dumps in three packets of sugar and pecks her cold lips at the rim. It's hot and sweet and feels like salvation and despite the scalding heat, she drains half of it at the milk stand.

She steps back to the counter and taps down her knuckles.

Hey Becky, she says.

Becky turns and edges up to counter. Is everything ok with your drink? She asks.

Yeah, its fine, I just want to ask you a favour.

Suspicion in Becky's eyes but her nature is honest and she likes this ragged girl with swabs of dirt on her face and a playful smile.

Ok, she says.

Can you give me an empty cup and the pen?

I can, but why?

I just want to leave a little message for that guy at the table.

Becky looks at the man, and then nervously around her.

Hang on. She pulls a cup off the tower, then a marker from her trouser pocket and places them on the counter and then looks at the girl with lingering confusion and moves back to the coffee machine to work the handles.

The girl writes a name on the cup and collects her own from the stand and marches to the door, diverting to the table to drop the empty cup on the table of the man with the newspaper.

He looks up grimly at the fresh distraction and then twists his head around as a blade of cold air runs through the doors. He looks back at the cup and holds it to his eyes and revolves it slowly to read the black scrawl.

Reads-with-a-Scowl, he says and looks back at the door but the glass has slid back across and the cup is light and empty in his hand.

Ten

FROM the coffee shop she walks the square and the arcade, perching on the ends of benches and low walls, bike stands and window ledges, she sits and watches for a minute before moving on. People shop in groups of two and four, swinging wide, square bags on thin strings and stop for coffee and lunch, pulling things from the bags to show them over the table to their friends.

Hidden in plain sight amongst them, in nooks and doorways and sitting with heads hanging against cold stone walls are huddled shapes, blanketed and inert, with faces of indifferent boredom. Too cold to fish for cash and pity they sit with their faces wrapped in dirty scarves and stolen hats, working the empty corners of tobacco pouches and sucking cold coffee from yesterday's cups. Ghosts of flesh, they are here and everywhere and nobody sees a thing.

The girl studies them all as she sits. She watches them watching the shoppers and the shoppers watching their feet as they pass them by. She eats the pastry from her pocket and moves on, drifting up past the river and then through the docks before returning to the square. She lays down her bag and pulls the sleeping sack tight around her shoulders and sits on her ankles with her back against the glass of a betting shop to keep her jeans clear of the snow. What light the day could raise is leaching away, and the sky is a soft, speckled grey and the air is tame and still. Fresh snow is building above it.

From the other side of the square she hears the brassy twang of guitar strings and then the four chord strum of another Beatles intro. She smiles and stands to see him through the knots of shoppers and catches brief flashes of his burgundy hat and the end of his guitar dipping around as he plays. His plaintive voice rises and falls in the still air above the crowd and she wants to go and see him but knows she better leave him to his work. She thinks of the money tucked deep in her pocket next to the bracelet and is somehow both grateful and sad.

An outlaw flake of snow spins against the dark, pebble-dashed backdrop of the council building. Weightless and alone, it waltzes its way gracefully to the ground, pulled from the ashen sky on a slender thread of gravity. She watches its flight and thinks of the sycamore seeds she would collect with her brother from the big tree next to the canal and then drop from the bridge and watch them twist and glide into the water. She closes her eyes and holds her brothers face in memory, his child's face and then sees it shape into the face of the grown man of her last sighting of him and how much he was becoming their father. She tries to force the true face of her father into her mind's eye but the image will only come amorphously and then scatters out of reach.

When she opens her eyes a bulge is caught in her throat and she swallows against it twice. I'm forgetting it, she says and feels a panic in her chest and wonders why she didn't take a picture of him before she left. There was a boxful in the loft.

Fresh flakes are coming and soon the square is drenched in a hail of white. Children detach from their parents and twirl, wide-armed into the blizzard and stick out their tongues to catch a wet blob before being gathered and towed reluctantly to the carparks, leaving lines of dark shoe prints in the frosted field of white.

The girl stands still against the glass, letting the snow build on her shawl. The music dies mid-song and through the storm she watches the blurred figure of The Bard collect his cap from the ground, throw the guitar around his back and leave. Within five minutes the square is soundless and empty and the darkness is draping around her.

She kicks some shape into her bag to use it as a dry seat and slides back down the glass to rest upon it. The snow bulks on her shawl and insulates her against a lifting, spiteful breeze that carries cold, wet darts into her eyes. The stiller I am…she thinks and sits and waits.

The lights extinguish in the shops around the square and the same staff she saw enter them at the start of the day fiddle at the locks and pull down the shutters and throw up their hoods and scuttle quickly past her. She's just another hump in the road, like the cobbles and bollards and benches that have been buried under the weather. Passive, inert and irrelevant. Made of the street itself.

She listens to her breath and watches it smoke and

disappear. It's slowing with every take and she's dipping into a lethal sleep when the voices stop in front of her. She prises open her eyelids, and stares at the shoes and the wet shine of the leather.

Are you ok down there?

Her eyes drift back down.

Hey, are you ok?

A woman in a black coat drops to her eyeline, hugging her knees. She has a honest look of sympathy and blonde tongues of hair that slide from her hat past her ears and curl under her chin like a strap. Somebody is with her, but all she can see is shoes.

The girl lifts her back against the glass and fissures open in the smooth carapace of snow across her shoulders.

What's your name, lovely?

Why does everyone need to know my fucking name, she rasps. What's yours?

The woman smiles. I'm Kerry and this is Phil. We're with the Salvation Army.

Are you gonna try and salve me?

Kerry laughs woodenly. It's just the weather sweetheart. When it gets this bad we need to try and get you off the streets. If you sleep here tonight you could have a problem. I'm sorry, but we have to try to find a better place for you to be.

I'm not sleeping here.

Oh, that's good. You have somewhere to go?

Yep.

Well, you looked like you were set for the night here. I'm not being funny, but you are buried in snow. If you stay here, it's really dangerous.

The girl groans and brings her hands from beneath the shawl to rub her eyes and then tries to stand. Her frozen joints are locked in place and she has to stretch her legs in front of her and flex them forwards and back before she can use them to lift herself up against the glass. She shakes off some snow and then whips the shawl from her shoulder and flaps it into the wind to shake it out before wrapping it back around her and closing it at the neck.

Phil has leather gloves and is creaking the fingers together.

Do you mind me asking where you are staying? He asks.

I don't mind you asking. There's an alley off Eastgate Street. I've got a bed stashed there and the alley keeps the snow and wind out.

A bed?

A mat.

He frowns. It's still on the streets though. We have to try and get you indoors when the weather is like this.

She stoops to collect her bag and starts to move off. Well, she says. I've been there for three nights already and the snow has been pissing down and you weren't out saving me then, so I guess I'll be ok.

Look, he says, and rests a leathered hand on her arm. We're not trying to get you to do anything you don't want to do. Council policy is such that when the temperature drops below zero they have an obligation to find shelter for everybody that wants it. I'm sorry we didn't see you before, but I can promise you we were out looking. This is the address of a shelter that will put you up for the night. It's called The Pembroke and I'm not going to bullshit you, it's not particularly great, but it's warm and dry and only a five-minute walk away. Can I give you the card with the address? It'll serve as your pass if you need to get in.

She holds his eye and nods. He goes into the inside pocket of his coat and retrieves a stack of small business cards and slides one off the deck. She takes it in her shivering fingertips and clutches it to her chest as she clasps the shawl back together.

Thanks.

No problem. It's what we're here for. Please don't sleep out here tonight.

She turns to leave and then stops.

Phil?

Yes.

You're alright Phil.

I know. We're just trying to help.

Can I have your gloves?

They both laugh. No, he says. I'll be out here all night.

Worth a try.

She turns and heads into the wind, lifting her boots clear of the snow as she exits the square onto an empty Eastgate. An oncoming car in the distance battles against the whiteout, its headlights sliding left and right upon the runway of ice as it struggles to find some traction. The snow charges though the white arc of the streetlamps like a tangle of insects and pieces of it fight their way into the girl's eyes and mouth. She is tired and hungry and her face is stinging from the cold and she's coughing as she hurries to reach the mouth of the alley.

Eventually she turns into it and squints as the light disappears. She stops and wipes a hand across her face and some primitive instinct cautions her against going any further. She stands against the brick and breathes and tries to quieten her breath. Her pulse rushes into her ears and throat as she steps heel first into an uncertain realm. At the pipework she feels for the cardboard mat. It isn't there. Blindly, she runs her fingertips up and down the metal pipes and then to the floor to see if it has fallen.

It's not here, she thinks. It's not here.

She sits back upon her calves. Her jeans are wet and cloying to her skin. She bores her eyes into the black depth of the alley and stifles her breath to listen and somewhere in the darkness a point of sound slowly develops into the rhythmic flutter of a snore. She leans further in and pads forward on her hands and knees and with the adjustment of her sight to the gloom she can see the outline of a body against the wall.

She watches it lift and fall in sleep and then it rolls and the scratch of a sleeping bag against the cardboard signals the end of her hopes. She stands and tramps back through the alley and into the street and lifts her face into the snow strewn wind.

Eleven

SHE stands on the pavement under the wooden sign of The Pembroke and watches it swing back and forth on the wind. It's clothed in snow but under the sickly light she can identify a faded sketch of some cliffs and a beach. Clumps of snow detach from the rim of the sign with every pass of the wood, adding to the mound piled around her feet.

Through hot, stinging eyes she looks over the building. It's a solid red brick block that was once a pub, with beer garden benches stacked against a wall and metal sheets bolted across the windows. Every instinct she possesses inclines her against going inside, but she cannot see beyond the bleak horizon of the night if she doesn't get out of the cold.

She crunches her way forward to the steps. Two lads sit working a spliff, one with the papers and gear in his hand, the other trying to form a barrier around him with the flaps of his denim coat. The kid with the papers wears a vest and he's not even shivering, rolling it with the calm precision of a surgeon. His veins run like blue wires inside his bony, chalk-white skin, and half-finished inkwork stops abruptly on his bicep. His eyes lift as she passes them on the steps and then back down to his lap.

At the door she doesn't know whether to knock or walk straight in. She stands for a second and casts another look back towards the street and then handles the cold brass knob and twists it around.

The sweet stench of dry vomit pushes her head back as she enters a hallway bleached in the light of an unshaded bulb. A red carpet runs under her feet and up a wide staircase that splits left and right at a landing. Doors stand off the hallway, closed shut except for the one by the foot of the stairs from where a television sounds and throws patches of colour against the creamy architrave.

A dog slathers behind the door to her right and urges her forward to the staircase. She pulls the shawl from her shoulders and lets it hang at her feet as she peers into the open room.

Hello.

A scrape of wood on wood and a wisp of a woman appears at the doorway holding her hands in front her. A greying bob of thin black hair is licked across her skull.

Yes, she says calmly.

What?

Are you staying?

I think so. I don't know how it works. Some guy from the Salvation Army gave me a card.

Yes. Do you have it?

The girl lets the shawl drop to the floor and finds the card in her coat pocket. The woman's thin fingers wrap around the card and hold it at a distance so she can read the number. Then she stares back at the girl without blinking, her eyes black and still.

I need to make a note, she says. Behind the girl a door swings open and someone barges past her and races up the stairs and is swallowed in the darkness. A scream and then another door slamming on the floor above. The woman's dark eyes follow the movement and then return to the girl.

I need to make a note.

Alright.

She glides back through the door and the girl stands under the buzzing of the bare bulb. Angry paws scratch at the door behind her and more doors are slamming above.

The woman slides back around the door frame with a key tied to a paddle of wood.

It's nineteen, she says and hands the paddle to the girl. Up the stairs and right to the end of the hallway, last one on the left. There's a toilet opposite. Do you need to go back out?

What?

Outside. Do you need to go back out?

I don't think so. Why?

I leave at ten and the door is locked until seven in the morning. If you're out when I leave, you can't get back in.

What happens if someone wants to leave in the night? Or if there's a fire or something.

The black eyes hover in their hollow sockets. I won't be here, she says.

Jesus fucking Christ, says the girl and throws the shawl over her shoulder and clumps up the stairs. She turns at the landing and the woman is still watching her.

She adjusts her eyes to the gloom of the corridor and

walks slowly into the abyss. A slot opens in the door to her right and the bushy silhouette of man's head, backlit from a red glow within the room watches her pass. She treads warily through the corridor with the heat of hostile eyes on her neck, ears taut for any sound that could indicate some movement behind her. She makes the end of the hallway and looks back up. A thin bead of red is at the open door still, the only colour in a chasm of black. As she stares the door closes slowly.

She turns and squints to try and find a number on the door in front of her. She lifts her hand and can finger read the metal of numbers one and nine. As she feels for a handle the red bead at the door down the passageway appears again. She finds the handle and turns it but the door won't budge. She tries to insert the key and it skates around the metal plate before sinking into the lock. The red bead is getting wider and she senses that the air is now being shared with another breath.

The lock clicks and she pushes through the door. Slapping at the wall she finds the switch and the room slowly fills with a buttery yellow light. She whips the door behind her and turns and locks it shut.

The room smells wet with decay and green patches of damp fan from the corners of the walls. A big oak wardrobe looms to her right and in the centre of the room a curved mattress leans over a metal bedframe. The window is barred and shuttered from the outside and on the floor beneath it a hole the size of a dustbin lid has been burnt into the carpet.

She eases off her pack and walks to the bed. Rust coloured stains run the length of the mattress in irregular swirls. She opens the wardrobe and then closes it back up and hears a faint metallic creak at the door and then turns to watch the handle slowly twisting round.

She holds her breath, watching as it turns and she senses the pressure being applied to the other side of the door. After three twists it stops and she breathes again.

I'm not fucking having this, she says.

She walks to the bed and pulls off the mattress and throws it against the door. She rattles the iron frame of the bed against its loose fitting bolts, then finds a coin in her pocket and drops to a knee to work the screws that fix the main leg of the frame to the side bars and footboard. As she pulls it away the frame collapses and she stands and holds the bar in her hands. It feels heavy and cold.

She collects her sleeping sack from the floor and shakes it out. The cover is still wet from the snow but the damp hasn't penetrated through. She zips it back into a tube and lays it down between the bones of the bed frame and the wall. She collects her bag and takes it over to the sack and rounds it into a pillow. She sits on the sack, unlaces her boots and pairs them neatly to the side. Next she pulls off her coat and lays it over the boots and then fetches the iron bar and lays it down next to them. With a final look at the door handle, she clicks off the light and slips inside the sack. I need to piss, she thinks, but knows she'll piss in the corner of the room before she goes back through the door into the darkness.

She pulls the metal bar closer to her and wraps her fingers around her nose to mask the smell of the room. A nameless dread visits her in the dark but she knows she can't sleep with the light on. She concentrates on the sound of her breath and wills the morning to come.

As she lies in and out of sleep a rolling tide of violence drifts around the thick walls of The Pembroke. A woman laughs mockingly in the adjacent room. A male voice begs for it to stop but only incites a higher plane of mockery and for a while the two sounds build upon each other, one taunting and the other shouting until it climaxes with the whump of a body thrown against a wall and a whimpering plea of forgiveness.

Doors open and slam shut and feet pound the boards of the stairways and halls. Dogs whine and howl and are kicked into submission then lie in wait to resume their madness. Police sirens scream operatically beyond the boarded windows.

With every sound the girl opens her eyes and lays her hand on the metal bar and always it seems that someone is testing the handle of her door.

Twelve

THE morning sky sits on smoky grey bands and then rises in a cold shield of blue above the city. Small black ticks of birds race across the sun-sparked rooftops and then settle and lift again. The girl taps the iron bed post into the ice at her feet and watches her breath range before her. Across the street they descend in ragged dregs from the steps of The Pembroke, slattern and stumbling and blinking into the sun, hands aloft to stem the hostile light. They clot on the pavement and shuffle around with reddened eyes, clutching plastic bags to their chests, bereft of direction.

She watches them with some residual anger and pity. Not so fucking brave now, she says and pushes off from the wall and up the street, skimming the metal bar towards the steps as she passes them. Her feet sink pleasantly through the crust of the overnight fall as she stamps out onto the main road towards the city centre. The sun is on her face and is melting transparent glassy edges around the snow upon the walls and steps and cars.

The square is crawling with people, alive to the

improvement in the weather. People are skating on an outdoor rink by the docks and queueing for space at pavement cafes.

The girl is hungry. She fingers through the last of Suni's money and calculates how far it will stretch. She humps her pack into a Burger King and buys a flat cheeseburger and a chocolate milkshake. She takes them to where the snow has been cleared from the library steps and where other people sit and lift their faces into the watery sunshine. Girls huddle to their boys and lay their heads on their shoulders and share a moment of unspoken peace.

A lad in a ripped summer windbreaker with uneven patches of hair on his face drifts from group to group with his fingers cupped in front of him asking for change. A pink inch of skin between the cuffs of his trousers and the black slip-on shoes where his socks should be.

The girl looks for his eyes as he stops in front of her but they are fixed at her feet. She places half a burger into his hand and he considers it for a second and then drops it to the floor and moves on to a couple perched on the edge of the steps and repeats his plea. They stand and leave. The girl leans forward and scrapes the burger back into the paper and takes a glace around before eating it.

She finishes her meal and balls the paper back into the bag and then sits and watches people pass through the changing draw of light as the sun moves across the rooftops of the square. When the rays find her spot she basks in the light and pulls the clump of tissue from the inside pocket of her coat and plucks off her gloves. She takes the bracelet from the tissue and lets it fall from the fingertips of one hand to form a golden coil into the palm of the other. She repeats this until the sun slips below the roof line. She lifts her head and watches blue banks of cloud ball and brood in silhouette on the horizon and around her the temperature of the air is falling.

The square begins to empty. The girl sits coldly on the steps and watches people leave and through the slowly moving crowd, she sees a bottle green coat slicing purposefully through the dense mass of bodies, a tail of black hair swinging from a high knot in time with each step, brushing the shoulders left and right. The girl throws up her pack and drops from the steps and weaves through the dawdling strands of people and falls in behind the coat. She's moving quickly, up through the arcade and down into Barton before she can catch at the green sleeve and tug it back.

Sun, she says. Hold up.

Suni spins around and wrenches her arm from the girl's fingers. She sees the girl and her eyes flare with recognition but her face is shocked and grey. She continues the turn and then stamps ahead, the black fountain of hair tasselling behind her.

The girl stops and checks herself. Suni! She shouts and quickens her step to fall in next to her, skipping to keep up.

Suni!

Not tonight babe.

Hang on. What's up?

Suni stops and turns around. Her eyes are wide and wet and ringed with tracks of smudged mascara. She looks up to the sky and then down to the girl and then begins to cry in staccato gulps, her hands up to her face to smother her grief. The girl stands open mouthed.

Sun, she says, her own tears pooling.

Leave it. I need to go.

What's going on?

The girl shouts unanswered questions at Suni's back and is left stranded in the cool loneliness of the street. New bits of snow blow through the streetlamps and stick to her hair. She drifts around the tangle of streets until she finds a bench and then sits there shivering. She knows it's time to find a dry spot for the night but her mind is running with worry.

She sits and thinks of all the things that Suni has done for her and all the help and kindness she has shown and deep within her a desperate need to reciprocate begins to swell. She needs to show her that she too has something to give, to prove her own value in this thing they share.

What would Suni do if it was me in a state? She asks aloud. She looks around the bench, and then shakes her head and grabs her pack. She wouldn't just fucking sit here, she says.

She stands and walks back through the shadowland of brick alleys and lanes, the falling snow already filling the footprints left by the day. Her own feet skitter on the ice as she walks and twice the same man passes her, inspecting her from the sides of his eyes.

At Suni's door she bangs her fist into the wood and looks both ways along the street. Silence and soft snowflakes. She bangs again and steps back into the road and looks up to the light at Suni's window, hoping to see some movement. In the darkness she hears the rising sound of footsteps chewing into the snow and a glide of panic quickens her blood. She leans back to the door and slaps at it with the flat of her hand and feels the shame of being there. She came here wanting to help but needs Suni to rescue her again now.

The footsteps are sounding faster and louder and are almost at the lamplight and she slaps again at the door and looks again up the street and is about to bolt when Camilla steps through the light with her lips formed into a scowl.

What are you doing here? She says, pushing her chin into the plush collar of her coat.

The girl is sweating under her hat and her breath is racing out in thin, white jets. She leans against the house between the window and door.

Camilla lights a cigarette. Are you alright?

Fucking hell. I thought you were some bloke.

What bloke?

Doesn't matter. I think he's been following me.

Camilla steps into the road and scans the street. She leans the spiked heel of her boot into the snow as she turns left and right, the red ball of her cigarette pulsing as she smokes and to the girl she looks stately and defiant and beautiful.

I can't see anyone, she says

Doesn't matter then.

You know I can't let you in the house.

I don't need to come in. I just wanted to see if Suni was alright. I saw her in town and she was all over the place.

Camilla remounts the pavement. She's lifting her chin to show a toughness but her eyes are moving around nervously.

She's not alright. Nothing is alright.

What's up?

Camilla flicks the cigarette into the ridge of snow in the gutter and looks up the length of the street again.

Did you see the news?

Why, what's happened?

Camilla leans in towards her. You know I can't let you in right? I'm sorry, but we just can't do it anymore.

I just need to know that Sun is alright.

She's inside. She's safe.

Safe from what?

Camilla pauses and lights another cigarette.

You know what we do, right?

The girl nods.

Camilla stares into the dark space beyond the girl and smokes, trapping it deep inside her and then letting it spill slowly from her nose.

I mean what we actually do?

I know enough.

Yeah, Camilla says.

So what's going on? Did something happen to Suni?

Camilla's face looks numb. Quietly she says, Sun's alright but one of the other girls…she didn't come back the other night.

How do you mean, didn't come back?

I mean she wasn't with us when we left.

And?

And then they found her the next morning.

The girl reels. What do you mean, found her?

What do you think?

What, dead?

Camilla smokes and nods. Her hands vibrating.

Fucking hell. What happened to her?

I don't know. She went up there with the rest of us and she was alright and then we had some drinks or whatever and went to work and I never saw her after that. Police found her in a layby on a country road and it was on the fucking news like, this afternoon.

She pinches the cigarette under the red tip and then drops it to the floor and runs her hand down her face and shivers and then punches into her coat pocket for keys. The girl stares into the street and then lifts her head sideways at Camilla, tiny crystals of white glued to the black hair under the rim of her woollen hat.

Cam, she says.

Yeah.

What are you gonna do?

I'm gonna make Sun a cup of tea and have a shower and go to bed.

Is she alright?

Camila grinds out a laugh. You know what Sunita is like. You better than most. She loves to take them under her wing and make a project out of them. It doesn't matter what I tell her. She had a soft spot for this girl. She wasn't even eighteen.

I don't know what to say.

Camilla holds her at the shoulder. She's got a soft spot for you too, you know that?

I know.

Well. I've got to get in.

Cam?

What?

What was her name?

Does it matter?

What are you gonna do?

You keep asking me that. I don't know. Nothing.

The girl takes a small step towards her. Doesn't someone need to tell the police?

Camilla closes her eyes and presses her fingertips against the door and shakes her head. Look, she says. If they didn't care enough about her that they let this happen in the first place you think they're gonna give a shit about me or Sun, or any of the rest of us.

She stands straight and then lifts her face to the pattern of falling snow. She turns and looks at the girl with eyes of wet stone.

I need to get in, she says. I'm sorry I can't let you in, I am. I don't know where you go and I don't know where you've come from but there has to be something out there better for you than this.

The girl holds her empty stare. I could say the same to you Cam.

Camilla turns the lock and as she steps through the door and closes it behind her, the girl is pulling her hat down past her ears and brushing the snow from her coat.

Thirteen

THEY are watching the dog creep closer. The boy says it's his but she can't see how he can make the claim. It circles away and then inches back towards them and drops to the ground and when it stands again its spine bends up like a bow being flexed and the skin of its back is so thin she wonders how it can stop the bone from bursting through.

What are you gonna do with it? She asks.

He shrugs. Just keep it.

It'll only hang around if you feed it.

He turns on the step to look at her, nearly offended.

I'll look after it, he says earnestly. I was never allowed to have a dog.

But you haven't got anything to feed it with.

I know, he says. But I will have. I gave it some crisps yesterday.

Dogs eat crisps? She asks.

He does.

She.

What?

It's a girl.

How do you know?

She laughs. You can tell.

That's alright, he says. I prefer a girl dog anyway.

She laughs again and draws her legs up under her coat and hugs them, looking at the ribs of the dog. Her own stomach is blank with hunger. The boy leans forward with his hands outstretched to coax the dog into coming closer and his fingers are chiselled white at the tips with cold. Razor sharp winds roam across the car park and the frozen snow sits all around them in hard grey shapes and the sky above them is grey and empty too.

Have you not got any gloves? She asks.

He shakes his head and grins at the dog.

What about money?

Nah. You?

She doesn't lie. A bit, she says. Not much though.

Are you gonna try and get some?

She looks balefully out across the car park. There's no point. No one's about. I sat out all day yesterday and I never even got enough for a tea.

I don't even bother no more, he says. I just nick it now.

You been caught yet?

Loads, but what they gonna do? It's funny how nobody fucking notices you when you've got your hand out asking but as soon as you try and nick something they can all see exactly what you're up to.

He says it to make her laugh but she doesn't. She stares up to the block of marbled sky above them and sadness lines her eyes. She kicks her legs out from under the coat making the dog skitter backwards and then stands and grabs her pack.

Fucks sake, says the boy. I reckon he was coming then.

She.

Oh yeah.

Are you gonna give her a name? Everything should have a name.

I definitely will. If she she'll stay with me.

I've got one for you. Not the dog mind. For you.

He looks up, puzzled. You know my name.

She smiles at him tenderly. A new one, she says. From now on you are Crisps-for-a-Dog.

What?

From now on introduce yourself as Crisps.

What?

Or some playful alternative, like Frazzles, or Skips.

You're off your head.

Maybe. She puts a hand on his shoulder to make him look up. Take care of her. And yourself yeah?

Where are you going?

There's something I've got to do.

Alright. He looks back at the dog. Come on girl.

She weaves a path through the car park to avoid the heavier patches of ice and heads up an alleyway that leads to the road. She walks down Longsmith Street, hoisting up her pack when it slips down the shallow curve of her shoulder and at the corner she stops and looks across the junction. The face of the building is a frozen waterfall of shining glass windows, each reflecting the same perfect rectangle of silver sky. On the pavement by the building entrance stands a tree, as tall as the building itself, with a black trunk and thick black branches holding armfuls of snow.

She walks across the junction and pushes open the door. Inside the air is warm and smells of stale food. A high counter with a folding hatch runs horizontally in front of her and to her right sit a line of chairs beneath the window. In the corner is a vending machine with a soft-focus picture of coffee beans spilling out from a brown cloth sack and next to that a small table covered with children's toys.

She sits at one of the chairs and likes how soft it feels. The door behind the counter opens and a policeman walks through carrying a cube of documents which he handles into a tray. He looks at her once and then back at the tray and then fiddles with something she can't see behind the wall of the counter.

Can I help you? He asks, his attention still on the desk.

She stands and draws off her hat and straightens her hair down her neck and walks to the counter.

I want to report something.

Now he's looking her. His look is doubtful.

Ok, he says, waiting for her to continue.

Is there someone I can talk to?

You can talk to me.

Alright, she says and shrugs with a little forged toughness.

I don't know how to make this sound any less dramatic but...I have some information about a recent murder.

His face doesn't change. That's fine, he says. Take a seat and someone will be with you in a minute. His eyes return to his desk. Hers are glued to the small, perfectly circular pink tonsure in his crown. He looks back up and points to the row of chairs with his pen.

Take a seat. Someone'll be out.

She sits and waits. He moves dutifully through his paperwork, pausing only to rattle the pen around his teeth. She can see him trying to snatch hidden glances at her from the above the high front of the desk. You're not very good at this are you? She thinks. Perhaps that's why you are on the front desk rather than out there investigating crime.

She looks at the drinks machine and the prices written in hand beneath each picture and sees she has just enough money left for a tea but knows it will be awful. As she wrestles with the thought a door to her right opens and a man in a blue jumper asks her to come through. The girl follows him into a small, white room with a table and chairs and there's another man standing in a white shirt with the sleeves rolled back past his elbows.

He smiles when she enters but doesn't offer his hand. The first thing the girl notices is how small the table is and how close they will be sitting to her and knows it must be weeks since she washed anything but her pits and crotch in a library toilet and how they must've smelt her from the minute she walked in and while this revolves in her mind, he's talking about names and she's missing what he's saying.

Sorry she says, slumping down in the chair. Can you say all that again please.

He leans onto his elbows and cups his knuckles with the fingers of his other hand. His forearms are covered in fine black hairs and his hands are thin and he tries to hide each one within the other self-consciously.

No problem, he says, but do you need to tell us anything before we start, concerning medication or drugs or alcohol.

She smiles thinly. I'm not high, she says. I'm hungry.

He nods. I can get you a tea, he says. Probably find a biscuit.

Before she agrees he bounces to his feet and slips out through the door. The one in the blue jumper is making a note on his pad. Then he looks up at the girl with something that might form a conspiracy between them.

He'll not be long, he smiles. Did you catch our names?

Yes, lies the girl. She doesn't want to give her own.

Good. Can we start with yours?

The girl shrivels in the chair. I'd rather not say.

He notes it on the pad. Have you got an address?

She stares at him calmly. No.

The other one comes back in carrying three plastic cups on the back of a thick book. He lowers it gently on the table and sits and places a cup in front of the girl, his fingers spidering on the hot rim.

Thanks, she says.

He blows onto his fingertips and looks down at the pad to where the other one is pointing with his pen and tilts his head.

So, you told our colleague on the desk that you have some information you'd like to share with us. Is that correct?

I just want to tell you what I know and go, she says, turning the cup on the table.

That's fine, he says.

Again she feels the reluctance in her throat, as if the information was her own sin to confess.

There was a murder about four or five days ago. Some girl got killed in the countryside. She pauses, hoping for some encouraging sign, but both men stare back at her blankly. She waits and forces them to break first.

Go on, says the one in the jumper.

She sighs. Well, I know who did it.

Their eyebrows steeple in interest.

You have a name? Asks the one in the shirt.

No. I don't have a name, but I know how you can find him.

Who?

The guy that killed her.

Let's start again. Tell us exactly everything you think you know.

Look, I'm not gonna tell you everything I know because it might hurt some friends of mine, but that girl was a prostitute, and there's a guy, or a gang of them that takes girls up from here to some country house and that's where she was killed. He takes them in a big silver van and drops them back off in Barton. That's all I know.

And you don't know his name?

No.

And you don't know where he lives?

No.

Registration number of the van?

She sighs again and feels defeated already. No

Or the address of this house where he takes these girls?

No.

Or even the village?

She roils about in the chair and starts to look for where she left her bag.

The one in the jumper attempts a sympathetic look. Have you ever been up to this house in this van?

Are you asking me if I'm a hooker?

No. I'm asking if you have ever been to this house yourself.

No.

The other one leans across him. How do you even know about it then?

Well, a friend of mine told me about it, she says. And I'm not telling you where she lives, so don't fucking ask.

They both tighten up and lean back in their chairs. The one in the jumper stops making notes and tosses his pen onto the pad. The other is winding his sleeves down the lengths of his arms.

Right, he says. Thanks for coming in.

Is that it.

Yes.

Are you going to do something?

Not sure what we could do, he says, pushing himself to his feet.

Are you fucking kidding me, she says.

He spreads his arms. Look, he says. You've given us no name and no address. You've told me that a man, or group of men murdered a girl you can't identify, known only to you by association and that you cannot divulge the names and addresses of those associates because they are prostitutes. You've given me no information with which to trace or investigate this man or men, other than they drive a silver van and can be found in the biggest criminal enclave of this city. And if any of this information turned out to be something that a criminal investigation could be built upon, we have no way of getting back in touch with you to call you as a witness.

She grabs for her bag and stands, her cheeks boiling with shame.

You make it sound like I did something wrong. I was

trying to help. Fuck this.

Blue jumper points her to the door and she flashes out into the corridor and then out through the vestibule into the street where the cool air is a balm on her hot and angry face. She stands and swears and stares back at the mosaic glass wall of the police building. Then she stamps her feet over a sooty ridge of snow on the pavement and marches back through the streets until she reaches the square and the arcade. She goes from shop to shop, stealing as much food as she can stash under her coat and daring them all to catch her.

Fourteen

THE weeks slide by and she huddles in her lair watching the days come and go. When she slips her hand into her jeans she can grip her pelvic bone like a handle. She does it often and tells herself she likes the way it feels in her hand. All girls want to be thin, she thinks and laughs a hollow laugh and when she laughs her reddened gums show their fragile hold on her teeth. She moves around on the mat to ease the pressure off her brittle hips and runs her hands around her neck and ribs and arms to scratch at the itch that never abates.

Things are simpler for her now.

No new snow falls, but the old refuses to melt and sits in clumps of tempered ice. The weather isn't cold, because there isn't any weather any more, just the unforgiving, changeless cold. The cold isn't going to leave and day and night are just variations of light.

On two occasions in the previous few days she woke in the night and felt another presence in the alley. She thought she heard a scrape of a boot and the rattle of smoke raddled lungs sipping at the frosted air but the hunger and the cold have dulled her senses to the point where she no longer trusts them. All of this bound to a lethargy that tells her everything will be ok if she just keeps still and sleeps.

She pulls the bottle out from between her legs and untwists the cap and tilts it to her mouth. The water trickles slowly over her tongue. She zips down the sack and lifts her feet clear and pulls herself up on the wall. She leans against it and stares out to the rectangle of metallic light at the end of the alley. A car passes through it slowly. She shifts up the alley until she makes the street and blinks around. The world is a monochrome swatch, leached of colour and life. She bends to a brown hump of snow piled against the kerb and scrapes away the polluted crust until she finds the whiter stuff beneath.

She scoops the snow into the bottle and tamps it down with a thumb until she has enough to make a drink in the morning and twists the cap around and shuffles back along the alleyway to the mat. She folds herself back into the sack and slides the bottle between her legs and lies in watch of the block of light at the end of the alley as it bleeds out to black.

That night she dreams of open country. She walks along a narrow road under a high afternoon sun that hides behind thick, foamy clouds. The hedgerows are fat with green summer leaf and the rocking pink buttons of wild flowers. To her left a field of yellow wheat stretches away, rippling in the breeze and the dark shadows of the clouds pass through it like ships. To her right runs a wooden fence and the pastureland behind it. This place seems known to her but she wouldn't be able to explain how. Horses stand in the field and nicker to each other as she passes. She uproots a clump of grass and shakes it at them but they only stand and stare.

When the numbness in her shoulder brings her back to the sepulchral dark of the alley, she twists in the sack and wills herself back to the dream. She can't remember the last time she dreamt.

She sleeps and then wakes again to more sore limbs and the sound of a muffled sigh and the sense of something out there. The darkness is lifting with the arrival of the dawn and through the grainy light she can see a denser mass moving away towards the mouth of the alley. She sits up in the sack and pulls the hair from her eyes and as she does she feels the stickiness on her face. Still stunned from sleep she runs her fingers across her cheeks and lifts up more of the tacky liquid. She rubs her fingers to her thumb and slides them together in the grease and then brings them to her nose and smells the bleachy tang of semen.

She erupts from the sack onto her hands and knees and heaves dryly. She tugs her fingers through her hair and globs of ejaculate string to the ground and her throat reaches into the bottom of her stomach for something to void. She gags emptily as the salt tears flash across her nose.

She staggers upward and runs through the alley, tripping on the loose cobbles, wiping at her face with the sleeve of her coat. She slumps to her knees at the bank of snow and plunges her hands into the frozen heap and pulls handfuls of it onto her face, scouring it into her cheeks and around her eyes and ears and chin. She's groaning and gagging on the cold soap as she forces it into her mouth and down her throat. She mashes clods of it into her hair and rubs it into her scalp and then leans forward onto her hands and knees as her body bucks in braying sobs.

A car creeps by on the hard white road and someone hurries nervously around her on the pavement. Eventually she stops crying and begins to sweep the mites of ice from her scalded cheeks.

She stands and walks the alley back to her bed. She sits on the sack and reaches into the bag for her boots. Her socks are wet and her feet are cold and numb. She peels off the socks and massages her wooden toes, forcing the blood in. She pulls the layers of sock apart to see if the inner one is dryer and when she finds it isn't, she pulls them all back on and laces up her boots. She closes up the bag and rolls the sack and ties it to the bag and stands and looks at the mat. Her instinct is to stash it somewhere safe but she knows she isn't ever coming back.

She drifts up towards the square with haunted eyes, her stomach a shrivelled pit. She feels the cold seeping through her clothes but doesn't shiver and the people that file past her eyeline beneath the dirty fur of the hood are just other bags of skin on the street.

She sits on a bench on the main road at the edge of the square. A cold mist rolls through the streets and the light is coming very slowly. She looks around and sees suffocatingly high walls of brown, wet concrete and grime smeared windows. Metal shutters pulled terminally across failed shops with bin bags stacked high in the doorways. People scuttle by with their eyes to the floor and their shoulders winched up to their ears. She thinks of her dream and the field of wheat and its endless horizon.

A bus pulls up to the kerb and lowers itself to release

a woman with a pram. The electronic board displays the single letter D. The girl stands and walks towards it, reaching into the inside pocket of her coat. When she makes the driver's cab she's fumbling open the screw of tissue to extract a folded note, taking great care not to lose the bracelet

The driver leans his forearms on the wheel and waits. She slowly replaces the tissue and straightens out the note.

Where do you go? She asks.

Sorry?

Where does this bus go?

It's a 'D'

That's not a destination.

He leans back in his chair.

Round the villages, he says. Burford, Moreton, round through Tewkesbury and back.

How much?

All the way back?

She nods.

Seven-fifty.

She pushes the note through the gap in the cab window. He slots it into a box and taps onto a pad and passes her the ticket. The door closes behind her and the bus shudders into gear.

Where's the change? She asks, wobbling around with the sway of the bus.

We don't do change, he says, swinging the wheel round as he glances into his side mirror. You should have paid by card.

She staggers down the aisle and stops at a seat next to the long metal heater on the floor and slides up to the window. She settles her bag down next to her and looks around. An old guy in a blue raincoat with a satchel on his lap is up by the driver and near the back, a girl with wires trailing from her woollen hat communes silently with her phone.

She reaches down to unlace her boots and slides them off. Then she presses the soles of her sodden feet against the warm metal of the heater, lays her head upon her bag and sleeps.

Fifteen

SHE wakes to the bus growling up a hill in its bottom sprocket. The road rises steeply through a dark wood and cuts up and back on itself at the elbows of the road and the inside of the bus is as dark as the wood and warm. She licks at the corners of her mouth and looks behind her. There's nobody back there and the man upfront in the raincoat has moved to a new seat behind the driver. He stares out of the window into the black crevices of the wood, his nose almost resting on the glass and smudging a patch there with his breath.

She watches him as she straightens herself up. She fingers the knots from her hair and picks at a dried lump with her nails. She thinks of the alley and pushes the bile back down into her belly. When she reaches down to her feet and feels the hot fabric of her socks she scrunches up her toes and runs her hand inside her boots. They're still wet so she tries to balance them on the heater but they fall under the movement of the bus. She stuffs her pack down next to them to hold them in place and then draws her feet underneath her on the seat. She can't remember the last time she felt so enclosed and dry and warm.

The driver is urging the bus over the crest of the hill and when they level out onto an open plateau the trees fall away and the bus fills with light. She pushes her face up to the window to get a better view of the fields. They're edged with snow but mostly rich and green and rolling up onto higher ground to be lost in the mist. The sun is there on the snow and the grass in pearls of clean light, dancing off the big, icy puddles that sit in the fields but the sun itself can't be seen in the sky. It sits above the ball of mist and filters through it, lifting the colour of the land.

Alternately the fields are dark with turned earth and long ribs of snow that lie between the ploughed ridges. The stone walls race past her nose and then dip and scatter to the ground in loose piles and then rise again and break at angles to border thin tracks that lead to clusters of honey stoned farmhouses and barns with slate rooves the colour of faded blue ink. Occasionally a crippled tree with silver bark sprouts from behind a wall and points its bare arms downwind and in the distance patches of forest hang on the higher slopes of the plateau, engauzed by the fine mist.

The girl is captivated by the depth of the horizon and the still and colourful palate of the land. She wants to get out and touch and smell it but the warmth of the bus holds her fast. It slows and stops at a wooden shelter by a church and a woman embarks with a toddler in a shiny one-piece suit. They sit near the man in the raincoat and he's kind enough to take an interest in the child and soon he's talking to the woman in an unguarded way. The girl watches and listens and wonders how they can be so casually intimate if they've only just met.

At another stop on the outskirts of a small town the man stands to leave. More people get on and the bus pulls into a lane of detached houses with prim gravel drives and glossy leafed bushes in full berry. When it stops again on the high street, the driver kills the engine and everyone but the girl alights. She sits for a minute and then leans out into the aisle to see what the driver is doing but he's hiding in his cab so she sits there, confused and staring through the window.

To her eyes the village looks manufactured and unreal. Tiny shops with pretty displays hung with fairy lights are wedged between medieval looking pubs with windows split into tiny frames of glass. The street is ordered and clean and everything seems to be exactly designed. The pavements are thick with people, but none of them appear hurried or stressed. She feels the pull again.

Quickly she stuffs her feet inside her boots and laces them up. She slides her arms through her pack and walks to the driver's cab. He's leaning on the wheel and tapping his thumb off the top of it.

Hi, she says.

Hello.

Are you stopping here for long?

Another five minutes, he says. I'm early.

She pegs her bottom lip with her teeth and looks through his window. Is there another bus? She asks. That does the same route as this one.

He nods and pulls up a strip of laminated card from beside his seat.

There's one at twelve and then another one at four-twenty.

And can I use the same ticket on those if I get off this one?

Absolutely.

She feels herself smiling. I'll do that then, she says.

He reaches down to the lever that opens the door and stretches a look over her in a way she would normally consider predatory but he might be just observing the tattered filth of her clothes and greasy hair and skin and when she meets his eye he tells her not to forget that the last one is at four-twenty.

When she steps off the bus the cold is quickly there on her hands and neck so she reaches into her bag for her gloves and pulls her hood up over her ears. She starts slowly up the street, tucked into the leisured sway of the tourists and ramblers and watches them closely. Parties of Japanese pensioners shawled in transparent plastic raincapes with heavy cameras leashed around their necks that pull their heads forward as they walk. Purple cheeked ramblers carrying ski poles and socks pulled high to their knees and young designer families with children in designer clothes. They all bubble and tide at the windows of boutique chocolatiers and antique shops and queue patiently to get in and then squeeze out from underneath the low door frames clutching small parcels wrapped in shiny paper. Every third place is a café or bistro and she can hear the roar of them as she passes, the nicks and scrapes of the cutlery on the plates and the surge of well-fed conversation.

She notices there isn't any snow or ice on the pavement and very little on the kerbsides. She thinks back to the rutted, icy footpaths of the city and the ugly brown stretches of snow rotting in the gutters and wonders if it's all been cleared away here to keep it looking nice for the tourists.

Halfway along the parade of shops she waits until a couple move from a bench and then she sits and looks back down the street. To her concrete scarred senses it has the artificial beauty of a snow-globe, or a scene from an old fashioned children's book. Something from the nineteen-thirties. She laughs at how much it looks like that. She thinks the people here seem calm and happy and although her unwashed shabbiness draws as many glances as it does when she's begging on the streets of the city, the eyes don't run away from her the way they do there. They hold her in curiosity and in some cases, pity. In the city the eyes ricochet and hide somewhere else until the owner can erase the memory of having seen her at all. She realises she isn't the same as all the other people in this place, but they all seem able to agree she exists.

She needs to eat. Her shrunken stomach doesn't complain anymore but she can feel her body turning in on itself and her mind is tired and loose. She pushes herself from the bench, crosses the road and continues on up past the last of the pubs and gift shops until she reaches a small grocers. She pockets a sleeve of biscuits and a small carton of orange juice and is amazed at how easy they are to steal. She wishes she'd stolen some more. She carries them to the bench and eats half the biscuits and then stows the rest in her bag.

The sun has finally burnt through the mist, and the snow on the signs above the shops starts to sweat and drip. The people loosen their scarves and fetch hats into pockets. A clock set in gold relief above a restaurant across the street gives her the time and she picks up her bag and heads up a street running perpendicular to the main parade, barely wide enough to permit a car and lined with tiny, terraced cottages squashed into tight yellow rows. She walks until she hits the open countryside and continues on a rise that lifts her above the village. Dogs bark from a farmhouse and above her the sky is becoming open and blue.

A footpath takes her across a field and then links her back down through the back alleys of the village to the main road. She sits on a wall by the bus stop and eats the rest of the biscuits in the sun. When the noon bus arrives she panics to remember where she put the ticket and then finds it in the bag and steps up into the bus. She walks to the long bench at the back and tucks herself up against the window.

The sunlight fights through the sooty glass and the idling engine throbs beneath her while the driver waits for his time to leave. The bus half fills and the doors swish across and they ease off the kerb and up the street. Her instinct is to sleep whilst she is cocooned in this warm corner of the bus but as it dips and climbs its way around the countryside and back to the city, she looks to a fixed point beyond the scrolling landscape, flint-eyed with resolve.

Sixteen

SHE works with a fervour. With a clean face and her hair
pegged back into a clip, she's up before the dawn and sits
through the day with her hand outstretched until there's
no one left to pester. No longer submissive and hopeful,
she's there outside the coffee shops, chipping away at
them on their morning run and then lively on the steps
of the bank later in the day, bouncing around, working
their guilt. She hangs around the doorways of the bars
and restaurants through the danger hours until midnight
and then exhausted, retreats to the suburbs and sleeps in
hidden niches. She wakes with the first gibber of winter
birds and starts again.

What food she needs and isn't given, she steals and all
the money goes into the pocket next to the bracelet. She
groups the coins and then exchanges them for notes at the
parking kiosk near the rugby ground. Within a week she
has what she needs.

She's unwrapping a muffin on the edge of a concrete
flower planter at the mouth of the square when she sees

Suni leaning against the shop window opposite her in her long, bottle-green coat. She's holding two cardboard cups and a repentant smile. A white shirt is tucked neatly into her jeans and her brown ankle boots flare beneath her skinny brown shins. Her lips are coloured a burnt red and as she smiles her teeth gleam with the same fulgent whiteness as the shirt. When she pushes away from shop, the girl expects the other models in the window to follow her.

Hey, she says

Alright?

You want a tea?

Always.

Suni passes her a cup and stands her own on the concrete lip of the planter and then folds the tail of her coat beneath her legs and pushes herself up. They peel off the lids in silence and pipe cool breath onto the tea. As they peck at the cups and lick at the hot spots on their lips they feel happy just to be there together and sense the same feeling in each other and want to prolong and enjoy it before someone spoils it with words.

It's warming up, Suni says, eventually.

Yeah.

Most of the snow has gone already.

Thank fuck for that.

I've been seeing you everywhere this week.

Oh yeah.

Yeah. Every time I had to go into town, you were somewhere at it.

The girl grunts.

More silence as the tea becomes cool enough to sip.

How come you didn't come over and say hi then?

Suni blows and shuffles herself up closer to the girl. I'm sorry babe, she says.

The girl closes the last of the space between them and can feel the soft wool of Suni's coat on her cheek. It's alright, she says. I didn't even know you were there.

I know you came to the house after you saw me in town that day.

I was just worried.

I know. Cam told me. I'm sorry I didn't let you in. It was...

Suni looks up the face of the building and her expression becomes shaded and weary. It wasn't a good time babe, she says.

It's alright. Cam told me what happened.

She was a good girl. Reminded me of you in a way.

Reminded you how?

Suni chuckles sadly and pushes the hair from her face, but the wind whips it back around her forehead.

Like, she had a soft centre, wrapped up in this hard shell.

Fuck that.

That's what I mean.

They both laugh, but it dies quickly on the wind.

What are you gonna do? The girl asks. You know you have to get out of this, right.

Suni grins bitterly. I know. I'm trying. It's not as easy as just saying it though is it.

Suni, you have to. Camilla too.

I know. We both know.

Like, fucking now though.

Alright, she says sharply, casting half a cup of tea into the concrete planter behind her. Spots of red are burning on her cheeks.

You don't know, she says, shaking her head. You don't know what it's like. You can't just say you're stopping and expect they'll leave you alone.

Why? Asks the girl, with the hardness of a challenge.

It doesn't work like that. It just doesn't. As far as they're concerned, they fucking own you and if you want to go, you have to go completely. Get out of the house in the middle of the night and just leave town forever. No trace.

The girl presses herself closer to Suni's arm. So just do that then, she says.

A sly grin pulls at the corners of Suni's full lips. She sits and waits, restraining the grin, unwilling to admit a secret, but knowing that it's coming out anyway.

We're gonna do it.

Really?

Yep. It's not just a case of leaving. You've got to have something to go to. We've got something worked out but we just need a bit more time. Just to put a bit more cash together.

Yeah, but what for?

You can't tell anyone.

The girl looks around. Who the fuck am I going to tell?

Promise you won't laugh?

Can't promise that.

Suni grins and then brings the flap of her coat over her knees.

We're going to open a dress shop.

What?

You heard me.

Where?

Back down in London.

What sort of dress shop?

It's like a second hand shop, but not for all the shit that people want to throw away.

What, the sort I wear?

Suni laughs and wraps her arm around the girl and almost pulls her onto her lap.

Not you babe, she says. I think you look gorgeous. A bit thin, but...

Alright. Leave it out. Whose gonna buy all that stuff anyway.

It's for rich bitches who have all these designer clothes they're never going to wear again, so they give them to us and we sell them on to other people who can't afford the originals and we get a nice commission out of it.

That's an actual thing?

It is. There's a place to rent in London with a flat above the shop. We just need a bit more cash to make the deposit.

How long will that take.

Suni swallows a breath and locks it deep down and then pushes it slowly back through her nose and studies them both in the reflection of the shop window.

A couple of months, she says.

The girl slides from under her arm in a quarter turn on the edge of the concrete sill and Suni turns in to meet her.

That's nothing though right?

Suni nods. Then she wipes a blemish from the girl's chin and folds a renegade tail of hair behind her ear and lets her finger drift down her cheek.

Why don't you come?

The girl's eyes round. To London?

Why not? It's only a two-bed place, but I could actually let you sleep on the sofa at this one. And we'll dress you in Balenciaga.

Nah, you're ok.

Why not?

I only wear Chanel.

Neither of them laugh.

Suni lifts the girl's chin to connect their eyes. It's not a pity ask, she says. I'd want you to come.

I know, and I love you for asking, but I can't.

Suni's attention drifts to a sheet of newspaper as it flaps past them on the wind. She looks at the cracked slabs and the remaining pockets of snow, running brown-backed through the gutter like rats. Look at this place, she says. What you gonna stay here for?

I'm not staying here, says the girl.

Suni starts to speak but then stops in thought. She slips off the concrete sill and stands in front of the girl, working it through.

You sneaky little bitch. You were already leaving weren't you? That's why you've been out working so hard.

The girl nods.

When?

Tomorrow morning.

She gasps happily. Where you gonna go?

The girl looks up the face of the building and then rolls her head to follow the upper floor windows until they meet the top of the adjacent block.

Not far, she says. Just out of the city. I just need to see more sky in the mornings, you know? More trees. Fresh air. Her face darkens. I'm done with this. I can't keep it up anymore. I was never meant to be here this long, I just…got lost. I don't know where I'll end up but I know if I stay here any longer… The words catch in her throat and she turns her face away as she tries to swallow them down but Suni is pulling her off the concrete into her arms and cradling her head against the down of her coat and stroking her neck as she cries. When she composes herself and pulls away, Suni's eyes are glassy and hopeful and proud.

I'm going to give you some money, she says, the heel of her thumb up into the corner of her eyes to stem the budding of her tears.

The girl shakes her smiling face. You don't need to, she says. I've got enough already.

Suni frowns. She starts to speak but the girl raises her hands.

Sunita, it's ok. You've done enough.

Suni face begins to crack and the girl reaches forward to her in comfort.

I could have done more, she says.

It wasn't your fault, says the girl. It wasn't your fault she died.

Suni looks around at the people walking through the square.

Maybe. Maybe not. Maybe its everyone's fucking fault. Maybe.

Suni swabs her face and pulls a line of mascara to her ear.

Be safe, she says.

The girl nods. You too.

Seventeen

EVERYBODY is working hard to avoid being caught. Curiosity compels their glances towards her but they don't want to forfeit the pretence of having seen nothing in the first place. When she looks up, they look down. The game is making her laugh.

When she woke that morning and crept into the daylight she felt something she hadn't felt for months. The heat of a sun's ray. Its wasn't much to behold, but it was there, a frail cushion of warmth on her cheek. She took this as a positive sign. She bought her tea and then sat outside at one of the tables to drink it rather than slinking off to a bench or wall. She drank it slowly and watched the shadows cower down the face of the buildings as the sun built above them and let her eye and mind rest upon the steps and corners and bike racks and all the other hard topography of the square.

She was hungry for breakfast but was driven by a greater need towards the laundrette. It was empty when she arrived. She walked to one of the big silver machines in the corner and threw up her bag. She pulled open the door and unzipped her coat, withdrew the screw of tissue holding the bracelet and then threw the coat into the drum. Then came the next layer, a grey hoodie and beneath that the red sweater. Then a long-sleeve cotton T-shirt and then a shorter sleeve, to leave her in a grey vest with grey lace trim at the straps and two tiny buttons on the chest. The third button was missing. She slid a hand down her naked arm to smooth the static hairs and then raised the arm to smell at the pit and quickly recoiled and closed the arm back down. She thought of Broken-Wing and if the wing had healed yet and then wondered if he was dead.

She sat at a plastic chair opposite the bank of machines and untied her boots. She peeled away the sticky layers of sock like wafers of prosthetic skin and flung them all into the drum. Then she stood and lifted her slender hips out from her jeans and balled them up and shoved them into the machine. She took her spare pair of pants from the bag and unclipped her bra beneath the vest and slid it out and threw them in.

Standing in black leggings and the vest, she slipped her hand inside the bag to a zippered pouch and withdrew a handful of coins. She walked to another machine on the wall and read the instructions and then pressed in some coins and took the sachet of powder from the slot and emptied it into the tray of the washer. She took her hat and gloves from the other chair and pushed them in and closed the door. She studied the instructions and then pressed for the right cycle and the door locked shut and water sluiced across the glass portal. She reached into the bag for the stolen library book, returned to the chair and rested her naked feet on her boots while she read

There's four of them now, playing hide-the-eyes.

A woman in her late fifties is folding sheets at the table, her disapproval signed with exaggerated sighs as she pinches her fingers down the folds of the material and stacks them, neat as paper.

Another woman sitting to the right of the girl, younger than the sheet-folder but tired and lined in the face, angles a look as her head bobs drowsily forward in the warm air. Opposite the girl a boy in his early twenties with a blond whorl of hair sits at the window, his bloody ears backlit by the sun. He can't prevent himself from lifting his eyes from his phone to the girl's nipples pushing through the thin vest. She could cover them with the book but doesn't.

When the drum slows from its spin and the door lock snaps, she stands and walks to the machine and throws the book up as the boy's eyes flood over her. She opens the door and reaches in to scoop the wet clothes into a ball and heaves them to the drier. She takes her bag off the top of the machine and drops it onto the chair beside her and checks again that she stashed the bracelet properly. She unscrews the paper so she can see the chain and gently twists it back up and unbuckles a side pocket of the bag to put it there. Inside the pocket she touches a unfamiliar packet amongst the lipstick and toothbrush and hair bands. She pulls it out and is holding a brown envelope, thick in her hand, like half a deck of playing cards. She glances up and the boy looks away.

Fucking Suni she mumbles, and the woman to her right stirs from sleep. She draws her thumb across the edge of the notes and knows that a lot of money is in her hand. Sneaky bitch, she thinks as a smile spreads up her face. Using the book as cover she checks inside the envelope again. Tucked up amongst the money is a scrap of paper with a phone number written in pencil.

She reaches back into the bag and unzips the inner pouch and pushes the envelope in. She sits back and picks up the book as her body tingles with the thought of what the money can bring. She thinks of Suni and feels a deep pull of whole and silent love for the only person to have cared enough to help her since she arrived in this town.

The woman has bagged her sheets and struts her way out through the door. The girl sits in thought until the dryer slows and stops. She opens the door and the hot air wraps around her and the clothes inside are as soft and warm as new life.

She dresses unselfconsciously, purring at the sacred warmth of the clothes against her skin. She puts the red sweater and the clean underwear into the bag and sits to tie the boots and then throws in the book and buckles up the bag. She whisks her hair out from the clip and pulls it all back up, the clip between her teeth and her eyes laying on the boy. He looks up and his cheeks stain. She stands and grabs the pack and winks to him as she passes through the door.

Despite the sunshine the air is cold and her breath is white before her as she walks to the bus stop. She sits at the shelter and pulls up her hood and waits. Across the street a girl no older than herself in unmatched boots and carrying a blanket roll beneath her arm shuffles along with a sore limp. She crosses the street and enters the square, sits against a wall and spreads the blanket over her knees. People pass and she lifts her head to ask a question. None of them respond. As more pass her by, she asks less often until eventually her head wilts onto her chest.

Watching her from the shelter the girl is searching for a name. She wants it to be something to do with the boots or the limp but it doesn't come easily to her and when it does the names are weighted with sadness and she realises the game is spent. She slips her hand into the bag and takes out a twenty-pound note. She walks over to the girl and stands her shadow over her with the note in her outstretched hand and the girl takes a second to realise what it is.

Are you serious? She says, hesitating to reach for it.

Yeah.

Thanks

You're welcome.

I won't spend it on...

Spend it however you want. It's yours.

She takes the note carefully. You're really kind, she says.

Not really, says the girl, thinking of the sheaf of notes in her bag. What's your name?

What?

Your name.

She opens her mouth to speak but then pauses and makes a tough face up at the girl.

Why?

I need to know your actual name.

She looks up the street and then down at the note in her fingers. Hannah, she says.

Alright.

What's yours?

The girl looks out from the square to the shelter. A bus sits in the traffic down the street.

Take care Hannah, she says and walks away.

Eighteen

THERE aren't as many people in the village this time. It isn't a weekend, she thinks. The same sort of tourists are there, milling about and spending money and bobbing their heads to appreciate one thing or another, just fewer of them and the place seems less artificial for it.

She is hungry and when she walks past a café or a pub she slows to look through the half-steamed windows and stops at one to read a menu printed in ornate black lettering inside a glass box on the wall next to the door. The door opens as people step past her and the fatty wafts of the food pull her forward but then she heels her feet and scans the menu again and looks up the street and moves on.

She makes three tours of the main run without committing to eat. She wanders into a shadowed lane until she finds the sun and sits on the floor against a wall. An old lady in a long camel coat and polished shoes with small, square heels comes into the lane pushing a wheeled shopping bag and when she steps into the block of sunlight where the girl is sitting, her smoky grey hair whitens. She tells the girl that she is glad it is getting warmer and the girl agrees.

She watches her open a gate and lift the trolley up from the pavement onto a low path and then pull the trolley behind her into her cottage. On the grassy bank by the gate are clusters of fading snowdrops, their white petal shells rusting in the sun and around them probe the thin, green fingers of daffodil, their tips beginning to yellow and firm into buds.

She lays her head on her arm and drops into sleep with the warm sun on her crown. She wakes to the smell of the newly clean fabric of her coat in her nose. She is happy in her clean clothes but she itches underneath them and when she scratches at her ribs her stomach moans emptily. She wonders if she will just steal some food from the shop again and then asks herself why when there is an envelope full of money in her bag.

She knows why.

She has money but no income. She won't beg in this place and isn't going back to the other one which makes the money in her bag a thing to be protected rather than used.

She looks up through the lane to the main street where things are pretty and ordered and safe and feels like a silly child drawn to something shiny and fun without knowing what to do with it but reminds herself that the people up here are unlikely to wank over each other in the street and that must count for something.

She walks back up the lane to the main village road and continues to the end of the row, past the bistros and chocolatiers to the least pretentious café she has seen. She pushes through the door into the warmth and the sweet, wet smell of almonds baking. People are finishing their lunches and dropping paper napkins onto their plates and they notice her as she closes the door and scrapes her boots against the fibre mat. A man reads from a hardback book in the corner and a curly blond child is drawing on a napkin from a tin of crayons with her tongue out for concentration.

The girl moves up to the counter by the glass with the cakes and pastries and salad boxes and wonders what to eat. She looks up to the chalk board on the wall and lets her desires unspool.

A woman comes through a beaded curtain and struggles to conceal her harried disappointment at seeing another customer waiting for service.

Can you give me a minute? She asks.

Ok.

The woman steps up onto a low stool to reach the chalkboard and places a red circle next to three of the choices and then drops back down and slides the stool back under the counter with her foot. She reaches into the glass display and rearranges the sandwiches and then looks past the girl to a customer and nods at something and disappears back through the curtain. She comes back holding two plates and switches them both to one arm and taps at the till and tears off the chuntering paper and bustles her way past the girl. When she comes back around she hits a button on the coffee machine and it starts to hiss.

Sorry, she says to the girl, and turns back to the machine and presses something else.

Busy? Asks the girl.

The woman turns back and tries to convey the depth of

her suffering in a single expression.

What can I get for you?

The girl looks up at the board.

What do the red dots mean?

It means we're out of whatever it is that has a dot next to it.

Right. Can I get some scrambled eggs and mushrooms on toast.

White or brown?

White. And a tea.

Pot for one?

What?

A pot of tea for one?

The girl looks around her. Erm, yeah. Obviously.

The woman flicks her eyes at her.

What kind?

What kind of what?

Tea.

Just tea. Normal tea.

She taps it into the till and then spins back to the coffee machine and works it and then places the coffee cups onto saucers and ladles them onto a tray and takes a small porcelain jug from a shelf and decants in some milk from the carton. She fills a tiny bowl with an even mix of brown and white cubes and places small silver tongs next to the bowl on the tray. The girl stands and watches the precise ceremony of her work and when the woman looks up she is surprised to find the girl still there. She commands her to a seat and swirls her hips around the counter past the girl with the tray balanced on her palm.

The girl sits with her back to a wall beneath a shelf

of books with worn paper jackets. She takes off her coat and stuffs it under the table with her bag. The kid with the crayons looks up from her picture and stares at her with the prolonged and uninhibited fascination forbidden to anybody beyond puberty. The girl pulls a face at her and the kid shows her the gaps in her teeth and pulls at her mother's sleeve to tell her about the girl and the face she made.

The girl looks out through the window and then at the table and runs her hand over the smooth, varnished wood. At the centre, a ribbed antique vase stands up three green stalks of a purple headed flower, belted at the waist with white string. She strokes the glass ribs and looks up to see the same display on the other tables and recalls a forgotten pleasure at the sight and touch of such pointlessly nice objects.

Her stomach is angry. She is accustomed to hunger but not in the company of finely scented food. Whenever the woman scurries through the curtain with some plates, she lifts hopefully in her chair and then settles back down when she realises it isn't for her.

It comes soon enough. A porcelain tea-pot with a metal lid on a hinge and a matching cup on a saucer. The tiny bowl of sugar cubes and the milk jug. The woman lowers the plate before her and lines the pots of salt and pepper next to the milk and everything is flawlessly clean and white.

The smell of the eggs builds beneath her. Slowly, she lifts her hand to the warm handle of the pot and pours a scalding brown stream into her cup. She curls in a thin bead of milk and a cube of sugar and stirs it all together. Then she taps some salt over the orange pillows of egg, speckled with herbs and tiny diced cubes of tomato and bobs her head to the plate. Her eyes drag to the counter where the woman is watching her with her arms folded over her apron.

She unwraps the cutlery from the napkin and starts to eat. The utensils feel clumsy in her hand but soon she is lifting great lumps of food into her mouth and sliding it down with the tea and hiding her burps with the back of her hand. She snags the woman's attention and asks for more toast. It comes with a miniature pot full of butter curls.

When she is finished her stomach feels painful and heavy but a sleepy, satisfied warmth is coating her blood. She hadn't noticed the room empty whilst she ate and now it's just her and the man reading in the corner. She remembers her own book and pats around under the table to find her bag and take it out.

The woman comes and clears the table and seems more amiable with less customers to manage. When the girl slips past the counter and into the tight corridor to use the toilet, she sees the woman in the courtyard beyond the kitchen, smoking a cigarette and staring vacantly into the flower tubs.

The girl sits to piss and unwinds a long reel of paper and cleans herself and tucks the rest of the paper into her jeans pocket. She returns to her table and asks for more tea. The street is darkening outside and the room is held in the temporary balance between the fading daylight and the sallow gleam of the café bulbs. The woman is wiping down the counter and glances up at the girl.

Closing in fifteen, she says.

The girl nods and drains the rest of her tea. She stands and pulls her coat from underneath the table as the woman cleans down the glass.

Hey, she says and the woman turns.

Is there anywhere to stay up here?

To sleep?

Yeah.

The woman angles her head to think. The pubs have rooms. And there's a guest house at the end of Coze Lane.

Are they expensive?

She shrugs. What's expensive?

I don't know. How much are they?

I wouldn't know exactly. The pubs are probably more but I don't know. You'll have to ask.

Ok.

She collects her bag. Thanks, she says as she opens the door.

The woman has turned back to the glass.

The street is cold and black-bellied clouds are closing out the sky. The shops are shut or shutting and the streetlamps yet to light. She crosses the road and walks to a golden pool lapped upon the pavement beneath the window of a pub. She asks at the bar about the price of a room and then walks quickly back out. She stands on the pavement and pulls up her hood against a trim breeze and the tiny flecks of rain it carries.

She walks to the edge of the village and follows a high brick wall up a narrow lane. At the end of the wall she stops at a gate and checks behind her. The wet air slips around her as she handles the gate and steps into an allotment, treading warily along the damp, grassy path. The black squares of sheds stand faintly against the purpling light and lighter shapes of plastic cloche sit between them on the bare earth. She walks silently along the path, twisting the handles of the shed doors as she passes them until one clicks open in her hand.

The air inside the shed is a mixture of dry soil and creosote. She fastens the door and waits for her eyes to adjust but becomes impatient and finger reads the shapes around her and clears away some tools to make some space on the floor. She unties her sleeping sack from the bag and rolls it out flat and sits on it to pull off her boots. From habit she tries to tie them up inside the bag to prevent them from being stolen in the night but abandons it and pushes them into a corner. She rounds the bag into a pillow and wriggles into the sack and pulls it up to her chin. She listens to the rain smacking softly upon the wooden roof and feels dry and warm. She claws her toes inside the double layer of socks and cups her hands around her full stomach and wonders how many people in the world could be as safe and happy in their beds as she is right now.

Nineteen

ON a low shelf beneath the window there are tins of paint and tubs of plant food and bottles of powder with chemical names. When the light becomes strong enough for her to read the labels from where she lies, she knows it's time to move. Nobody comes to an allotment in the dark.

For over a week she has followed the same routine. She rises with the coming light and collects her things and slips from the shed into the morning mist and out through the allotment gate. She buys a pasty and a box of juice from the shop and sits on a bench at the top of the main street and watches the buses deposit the tourists.

Then she takes a long walk up through the woods that climb the hill away from the village. She stops at a bridge in the valley to throw twigs into the stream and watches them nose out through the other side of the wooden planks where they spin in the shallow eddies at the bank and then catch on the current and race on through mossy rocks.

She follows the track back up through the fields to the village, stopping at a farm to admire an old chestnut cob with a ragged black mane, tugging at a hay basket bolted against a stone wall. She talks to it while it eats, and the horse lowers an ear to the sound and she thinks if she does this every day and wins its trust, it will come to the fence to be stroked.

At the village she buys herself a meal and some tea, rotating the places she uses in turn. There's three café's on the main street, all providing the same thing for the same price but she prefers the one she tried on the first day and would use it exclusively if she didn't think she would become conspicuous. She knows none of them want her there, with her tattered clothes and spotty face, but the owners of the other two places annoy her with their phoney welcome and plastic smiles of sincerity.

The woman in the first café seems genuinely irritated by everyone and everything and tolerates the girl with very few words exchanged between them. The girl prefers the integrity of it. She uses the toilet, pays her bill and sits in the street until the dusk starts to wash up over the plateau. Then she returns to the shed.

This morning is colder. She has her knees up to her chest in the sack and her breath is curling out from her nose beneath her hat. A marbling of frost covers the inside of the window and the paint labels are slowly coming into focus. She knows she has to move but the cold persuades her to stay for longer than she should. She sits up and hears a wooden creak outside the shed. She holds her breath and strains her neck up to the window.

Something is humming.

In small sections of movement she peels back the sleeping sack and pushes her feet into her boots. She stands up and onto her toes to see through the frosted glass, her fingers resting lightly on the shelf. A brown shape sits just beyond it and the humming starts up again.

Fuck, she says, and screws her eyes shut.

She stands thinking and then touches the cold metal of the latch and lifts it up and probes an eye through the crack in the door.

The man is sitting on the bench beneath the window in a brown cord cap with padded gloves cradling a silver cup of something. He sucks at the cup and stares out over the frozen earth.

Morning, he says.

She pushes the door forward another inch.

He turns to look at her and then back at his cup.

Nice morning.

She leans through the door and her face meets the cold air.

He turns again and runs a gloved finger through his white moustache. You want a bit of tea?

Ok, she says.

Get a cup from in there, he says, pointing the finger back at the shed. There's a box on the table by the vice. Should be one in there.

She withdraws into the shed and opens a wooden box on the table and finds a tin cup amongst some bags of tea and sachets of sugar. She notices a small, red pocket-knife on the window sill and stretches forward and folds her hand around it. She bends to pick up the sleeping sack and wraps it around her shoulders and goes back through the door and holds out the cup.

Get yourself a chair, he says. They're not very clean but

I don't think this bench will hold the both of us. It's on its last legs.

Back in the shed, she lifts a folding chair from a hook next to a lawnmower and carries it out. She snaps it open and settles it onto the stiff blades of grass, angled to where he sits on the bench. He pours some tea into her mug and hands it over.

There's sugar in the box, he says. She wants some but doesn't want to get back up. She tucks the knife between her legs to allow her hands to take the warmth from the tea.

He thumbs up the peak of his cap and pulls his scarf around his neck and smiles at her with hazel eyes in watery pink sockets. The smile folds the skin of his cheeks back to the clipped white boards of hair running in front of his ears.

Why are you sleeping in my shed?

She stares at the tea in her hand.

It was only one night. I'm sorry.

Better not to fib about it, he suggests. You've been here since Wednesday.

She stares at the cup.

He dips his moustache into his tea and sucks off the drops.

Didn't think I knew that did you?

She lifts her shoulders.

Old souls like me get up very early in the morning, despite having very little to do.

You're not that old.

You get points for that, he says and gives her a gold tooth. Still doesn't explain what you're doing in my shed.

She shuffles around in the chair and as she opens her

mouth to speak he holds up a hand to quiet her and points it out over the allotment.

See that?

What?

On the spade. Big fat bugger.

She looks to the spade where a robin has perched, twitching its head around its plump ginger neck and belly. It's spidery claws are throttled around the wooden handle, finely balancing his rounded body.

Don't know how he manages to fly, he adds. He comes for worms when I turn over the ground. You were going to say something?

She is still and contemplative. I just needed somewhere warm to sleep, she says. I can't afford a room in the pub. Well, I can, but not for very long. I'm sorry for taking the piss. I'll just get my stuff and go.

Where are you going to go?

Doesn't matter. It's ok. She stands up from the chair.

Sit down, he says, lowering her back into the chair with a movement of the glove and shaking his head thoughtfully, like he needs to find a better way to explain some elementary concept she isn't able to grasp.

He tops up his cup from the flask and places it on the arm of the bench. He looks up at the pink frosting of the sky in the east and says, I don't need to know your business and I'm guessing you haven't the mind to tell me. You can't stay in my shed though. If I were to let you stay I'd have the responsibility of knowing that you were here and if you froze to death one night…well…that wouldn't benefit either one of us.

I've slept in much colder places than this.

Hardly the point I'm making.

I'm not saying I should stay. I'm just saying. I'm not going to freeze in there.

Where have you come from?

I was in the city

He pushes his lips up to the middle of his moustache where some lines of reddish hair still survive amidst the bristles of white and when the girl looks closer she can see the same red traces in his sideboards and again in the neatly clipped hair below his cap at the neck. He claps his gloves together for warmth and the robin bolts from the spade handle into the hedgerow.

I don't want to sit here and interrogate you, he says. The wife would. She does the talking for both of us which saves me the bother. You seem to be alright but I have to ask. Are you in any trouble?

No.

Good.

Will you tell her?

The wife? He recoils in mock horror. I'd rather not have to explain why I'm keeping a young girl in my shed.

She laughs and the knife drops through her legs onto the grass. She slides her foot over it and drinks the tea and watches him drain his cup. He flicks the dregs out onto the ground and screws it onto the flask and prises himself to his feet.

Nice plot here, he says. Gets the best of the sun in the summer and autumn and it's protected from the wind tucked up in the corner by the hedge and the wall. I put tomatoes up against it and they do alright. Better in a greenhouse, but we work with what we've got. What are you working with?

She feels a protective veil lifting inside her but isn't ready to confess her secrets.

Can I sleep here another night? She asks. I just need to work a few things out.

He nods. I think we can manage that. Would you like another call in the morning or shall I leave you to get on with it?

Still wrapped in the sleeping sack, she stands up from the creaking chair into a thin layer of sunshine gliding over the allotment wall which brightens her face.

I'd like that, she says.

Twenty

SHE stayed for more than one night. He was there in the mornings with the breaking of the night and woke her with his sad and softly hummed melodies from the bench beneath the shed window. The mornings were hard and clear and she would see the paling stars flicker against the pastel dawn colours when she carried the chair from the shed and took the steaming cup from him. On the third day he bought her cold toast wrapped in stiff brown paper and some fruit. He would complain that she couldn't stay but never officially pressed her into leaving. He talked to her about the plot and when to get the first potatoes in and how the snow over the winter was like a good layer of manure and then about his son who lived in Berlin and didn't visit as much as he should because of his work and how this made his wife feel.

She liked to hear him talk about the seeding of his plants and the rotation of his beds and was glad of how he never questioned her about her past and what she intended to do. By avoiding the subject of her life and her plans for the future, he coaxed her, unintentionally, into releasing fragments of them into the stream of their conversation like bubbles floating to the surface of a gently simmering pot.

The rain blew up eventually and she wakes one lank and sodden morning to find him late and tapping at the door in a green oilskin coat with a brass zip. She stands up from the sack and opens the door, aching and tired.

Come on, he says. I'll buy you some breakfast.

Still numbed by sleep, she slips on her boots and pulls on her coat and goes into the bag for some money. She catches him up by the allotment gate and they push their heads through wet strobes of wind until they meet the main village street. She always enjoys the stillness of the village in the morning before the crowds arrive and she senses the people who live and work there appreciate it too. They sweep the patches of pavement outside their shops and let slip their opinions on the village news. Then the buses arrive and they don their masks and go to work. Today the weather is keeping them all indoors.

He is more limber than she thought and she hustles up the street to keep in his step, the vintage shop signs swinging on the wind above their heads. They make the café and he opens the door to let her in and follows behind her. It's empty and fresh coffee is roasting. He unzips his coat and hangs it with his scarf and cap on a stand by the door and pulls a chair from a table by the wall and hitches his trousers at the knees to sit. The girl stands uneasily by the doorway.

Are you sitting down? He asks.

She creeps to the table and lowers herself into a chair, her eyes on the beaded doorway to the kitchen.

Take your coat off, it's wet through.

I'm alright.

The woman comes through from the kitchen carrying a vase of white lilies and her habitual air of persecution. Her step stutters at the unfamiliar sight of the girl and the man together, or maybe the sight of the girl at this early hour, but she shrugs it off and places the flowers at the end of the counter.

Morning John.

Nancy. Lovely flowers.

They are. Why are you here so early?

We'd like some breakfast if you've got a minute.

She blows and pats around her pockets. She finds the pad and licks the pencil tip and asks them what they want.

Just a tea for me, he says.

I thought you wanted breakfast.

I had mine hours ago. She'll have the full English though. He turns to the girl. Full English do you?

The girl realises she is scowling and corrects it.

Just some tea and toast please. I'm not that hungry.

White toast?

Yes please.

The woman tosses the pad on the counter without having written on it and turns out through the door.

John lays his hands on the table and laces his fingers together, spinning the thumbs. He leans into the girl with a slender grin.

Nice girl, Nance, he says. Bit spicy mind.

She returns the smile. I like her, she says. I come here sometimes in the afternoon.

Good, he says. That'll help.

Help with what?

He turns to the rain soaked window. Look at that, he says. Filthy. Should keep the sightseers away.

She unzips her coat but leaves it on.

Do you mind them? I mean, does it bother you that your village is always full of tourists?

Not really. Tourists are always happy and I like to live in a place where people are happy to be there.

I know what you mean, she says.

The woman comes out with a tray and starts to unload the cups and miniature jugs and bowls. She reaches forward to hand the silver toast rack to the girl with a sarcastic look in her eyes that tells of the many questions her mind is asking.

Thanks, says John. Can you sit for a minute?

Nancy looks back at the counter. Not really. Why?

I want you to give this girl here a job.

Both women baulk.

I don't want a job, says the girl, the scowl rushing back.

I haven't got any jobs to give.

He raises his hands.

Hear me out, he says and they both rush to talk again.

He points to the girl. You. You can't live in my shed anymore. If the wife finds out I'll be sleeping there myself, but I'm too soft hearted to kick you out and I think you know this.

Nancy's eyes lift. She's been living in your shed?

The girl throws cold blades at her.

And you. He turns to Nancy. You're rushed off your feet here every single day and forgive me for this, but I know it's because you can't afford to pay for the help you need.

She glowers at him, tight-lipped.

He draws a breath and pours out the tea. Now, he says. You've got the place out the back you are converting into guest accommodation and I know it's not finished but she's not that fussy.

The girl turns the blades on him. Thanks.

If she can stay there until the summer she'll work for free.

Hang on, she says.

I can always start charging rent on the shed.

She concedes and drinks her tea and plucks some toast from the rack.

Nancy is holding the tray against her belly and shaking her head but more in query than rejection of the idea. She starts to speak and then stops and looks over the girl and taps at the tray.

I'm not being cruel love, but you're living rough. You've obviously got some money to come in here and eat, but I don't know you, or where you've come from and this business is all I've got. I'm not going to pretend that I don't need the help but I'm sorry John, I'm going to say no.

He strokes at his moustache. I don't blame you for that. But remember when you first came up here? You needed a bit of help. She needs a bit of help now. Besides, I'll vouch for her. If she robs you blind, it's on me. I'll see it right.

The girl is gaping at him and her heart is throbbing under her vest. The toast is dry in her mouth and she drops the bread back onto the plate.

Nancy takes the tray up to the counter and slips behind it to work at the coffee machine. The café door opens and the wind roars in. A teenage boy in a black shirt goes to the counter, raking the wet from his hair.

The girl is still trying to choke down sticky clods of toast.

John pinches a cube of sugar from the bowl and crunches on it and sips at his tea.

You want to ask me why, he states patiently.

She bobs her head.

Better not to make a fuss about it. Let's just say I want my shed back. You're a nuisance.

She's not gonna let me work here. Look at me.

Maybe. Let's see.

The teenager leaves with a paper bag full of pastries tucked up under his arm and Nancy follows him to the door. She closes it behind him and stands with her hand on the glass pane and looks up at the rain dashed sky. After a minute she comes to their table and pulls out a chair and sits down and looks keenly at the girl. She rests a hand on John's arm.

This is a good man.

The girl nods her agreement.

Have you ever worked in a café before?

I worked in a hotel kitchen for a bit. Washing dishes.

That's a start. I can't pay you anything but if we can finish up the plumbing in the guest house you can stay there until the summer season and then we'll have a think about it.

The girl's lips are twitching.

What needs doing with the plumbing? Asks John.

It's all there, it just needs connecting. The toilet, the shower.

I know a bloke owes me a favour, he says. I'll give him a call. He slides a triangle of toast from the rack and leans over to the girl and wrinkles his nose at her.

A shower is the first thing she needs, he says and lifts a yellow edge of butter up from the miniature bowl with his knife.

Twenty-One

SHE still wakes with the dawn. She is entitled to sleep through it but when the light starts to shift in the courtyard through the unshaded window of her room she rolls awake and knows she won't return to sleep. She reaches out from beneath the duvet to the stool and lifts up the bracelet and winds it around a finger. Then she sits up against the pillow to see through the window, above the high wall that borders the garden to check if there is any rain about. The sky is a luminous blue with traces of fine, white cloud brushed up into the stubborn dark depths of the retiring night. She thinks it might be warm again.

She puts down the bracelet and clicks on the lamp by the stool. The walls are bare and brown except for six lines of colour on the wall by the door, daubed across the open plasterwork. The tester pots an untidy heap on the floor. She likes the sage green but isn't being consulted on it.

She swings her feet from the bed and yawns and shivers. She walks the wooden boards in her pants and t-shirt to her bag and kneels to the block of folded clothes and slips out a jumper and some jeans and throws them onto the bed. Then she goes to the bathroom and runs her hand under the tap and cups the cool water to her face and wipes her hand across her cheeks and takes a mouthful to drink. She walks back through the bedroom into the darkened living room and sits on the sofa to pull on her clothes. Towering cardboard shapes bound with plastic cord loom behind her in the kitchen space – a refrigerator, cooker and dishwasher ready to be unpacked and connected.

She takes the key from the arm of the sofa and holds it in her hand like a heirloom. She presses the flesh of her palm around it and opens it back up. A key to lock a door behind her while she sleeps. Her key.

She unlocks the door and plants her naked feet onto the cold flagstones. The air is mild and still and freckled with new green smells of grass and growth and she feels the swell of spring bubbling up through the soil and leaching through the grey stone walls around her. Everywhere the silhouette of flower heads are starting to lighten underneath the chalking of the sky. The bearded racemes of unopened wisteria droop over the back door to the café and the black, coronet heads of tulips, lofted from the tubs on their tall, skinny necks, lie in wait to burn pink and red and orange under the noon sun.

She walks the path between the raised borders with an arm outstretched to collect the dew from the shrubs on her fingertips and then stops at the gate and pulls her hand through a clump of rosemary and brings a cup of scent to her face.

The bathroom window on the upper floor above the café flares with light and she is reminded of why she is there. Nancy's blurred shape swims around behind the glass and then the light shuts off and the building sits in darkness until the white, sterile tubes of the kitchen flicker into life and create crisp new shadows around the girl's bare feet on the courtyard floor.

She slips unseen back into the guest house. She knows she has an hour or more until the back door is unlocked so she begins her slow, meticulous journey through her favourite event of the day.

First, she takes a towel from the top of the door and carries it to the bathroom and lays it over the middle spoke of a chrome plated radiator fixed onto the wall next to the shower. The heating isn't plumbed in yet but she measures it precisely over the polished bar, ensuring the edges tailor at the bottom. Next, she pulls the red sweater over her head and hangs it over the back of a wooden chair in the corner and does the same with her jeans and t-shirt.

Above the sink a mirror and a rectangle of plastic. She pulls the cord and the peachy light shines her face and neck and breasts. She stares into her own reflection and tightens her jaw and pouts to thin her cheeks and leans her face in towards the light to see the open pores and the fine black wisps of hair above her lip. She stands on her toes and arches her back and looks down her body as far as the mirror will allow and swivels on the balls of her feet to bring her body into profile.

She crouches to her knees and opens the cabinet beneath the sink and looks at her new things. She lifts out the toothpaste, brush and deodorant she bought at the village shop and then the creams and potions John gave her when she first moved in. He claims they were donated by his wife, but she suspects they might have been stolen. They mostly smell of lavender.

She places them all at the back edge of the sink and goes back into the cabinet for the tweezers and there her hand finds her old toothbrush with the cartoon characters and splayed bristles. She moves to throw it into the metal can by the sink but stops and runs her thumb over the head and doesn't want to let it go. She puts it back and then nips the tweezers around her upper lip and eyebrows and drops it ringing into the sink. Then she takes the toothpaste and new brush over to the shower and slides back the door and twists the cross of steel and watches the water blow from the head in a solid tube of water into the tray. She slips off her pants and stands and listens to it sough and waits until the glass starts to steam and then steps in.

She stands under the head with her face into the jet and lets the hot torrent rush upon her hair and skin and swaddle her in its purifying, protective energy. People shower every day, she thinks, but don't know what it is to be dirty. She washes and conditions her hair and fingers a gritty scrub into her nose and cheeks and stands and lets the water wash away the sticky memory of alleyways and dusty sheds and grimy sleeping sacks. She takes a plastic safety razor from a tray and glides it up her legs and raises her hands to take it underneath her arms and then brushes her teeth slowly. Her fingers wrinkle and she picks beneath her nails. She stands there for a long time.

Eventually, she twists the metal cross back around and opens the door and shivers for the second time that morning and smiles at how soft and pampered she is becoming. She pulls the towel from the rail, wraps it over her chest and wipes a watery smudge through the steam upon the mirror and scoops some lavender cream from a pot and smoothes it into her face.

In the bedroom she dries herself and blows her hair and ties it back and dresses. Nancy insists she wear the black trousers, white shirt and pumps she found for her and the girl wonders, as she always does, why she wants her to dress as a waitress if she won't let her out of the kitchen. She laces up her pumps and kills the lamp and steps out into the courtyard. The door to the kitchen is open and Nancy is smoking on the bench beneath the window.

You smell clean, she says, tapping the cigarette butt into a flower pot.

Good, says the girl. Is the bread here?

Nancy pushes herself onto her feet. Just now, she says and yawns. It's by the door.

The girl steps into the kitchen and then through the corridor and into the muddy light of the café. At the door she lifts the wicker basket full of long, paper-wrapped loaves and carries it back to the kitchen and slides it onto the counter. She squints at the list taped to the wall and starts to unload plastic tubs from the fridge and peel back the lids.

Nancy watches her from the door. Make us a tea will you, she says and takes one of the tubs and replaces the lid and returns it to the fridge. Don't worry about the brie and cranberry. The brie didn't come.

The girl fills the kettle and starts to unwrap the bread. She cuts the loaves and washes the salad leaves and sits them on the sink to drain. She peels slices of meat from waxy paper and knifes through cheese and builds the sandwiches into pyramids and then wraps them back up. She carries them through the beaded curtain and lines them up behind the glass on the counter.

She drinks her tea and starts to unload the crockery from the washer and stashes it onto the shelves. Twice the older woman comes back through the beads with a baguette in her hand and puts it on the table with a critically raised eyebrow demanding a better effort.

Soon the doors are open and the noise from the café starts to gather. Her duties are simple and unvarying. Nancy brings the trays of dirty crockery in from the café and puts them on the counter. The girl loads and empties the dishwasher, putting the clean things on the metal rack by the door to dry. She fries bacon and boils beans and makes more sandwiches and rounds of toast and fills the miniature pots with butter and jam.

When she has an idle moment she makes herself a tea and stands at the window to listen to a radio turned low on the sill and looks out to the garden. At lunch the rush begins and she sweats to keep up with the demands being made upon the kitchen but by three o clock the place has emptied and Nancy lets her leave. Sometimes she walks with John or walks alone. She returns at five to give the kitchen a final clean and then her work is done.

As the evening light lengthens, she watches Nancy pottering around the garden through the window or the open door of the guesthouse. At night she lies on the sofa and reads the books she has borrowed from the shelf in the café and falls asleep with a book on her chest. She wants to ask about a television but doesn't want to ignite a conversation on how long she might be staying. When she thinks about having to leave, she always thinks about the shower.

Twenty-Two

THE sound of John humming beyond the gate at the end of the garden. She always hears the humming before she opens the gate and is always glad to hear it. He's holding a stick of polished wood and has small field binoculars hanging around his collar.

Alright? She smiles.

He looks watchfully around the sky. I am now the rain has let up. How long have we got?

Couple of hours, why?

Feeling fit, he declares. We'll push on a bit today if you reckon you can keep up.

I'll manage.

They walk the back lanes of the village, parallel to the main street and then up past the allotment and into the open country. They take the road up a rise and the sun lances through the scattering clouds and makes the wet road shine like poured metal. Around them runs the pulse of resurgent life. White blackthorn blossom blazing in the hedgerows and a maze of swollen buds pushing through their waxy seals. Tongues of fern unfurling in the shade of the pine woods and the wet, peppery smell of freshly turned earth. As they walk, tiny birds chase across their path and brake on stone walls and sing and split again and always the rhythmic tap of John's stick measuring his step.

They leave the road over a stile into a broad heath dotted with clover and the lilac snouts of wild orchid and as they break the peace the rabbits bolt over grassy humps to find safety in the circular stands of gorse.

They follow the incline of the heath up towards a wood and pass through it over the ridge, the muddy path flanked on either side by oceanic drifts of bluebell. They emerge from the wood into the broad panorama of the valley and a fallen oak to sit upon and take the view. John fumbles into his coat pocket for some chocolate biscuits wrapped in foil and hands a couple to the girl.

What are the big blocks of yellow? She asks, pointing a crescent of biscuit to the shimmering fields across the valley.

Rape.

It's what?

They're growing rapeseed for the oil.

It's pretty.

He nods. How are you getting on in the guesthouse?

She nibbles at the biscuit and thinks about the question.

She starts to speak and stops and sighs. John turns to look at her on the log. She sucks some chocolate from her thumb and studies her fingers.

It sounds stupid to say it, she says, softly, but it's like....

What?

If I admit to myself how much I like it there, it'll just make it worse when she makes me leave.

Why do you think she'll make you leave?

Couple of reasons. One she wants to rent it out to people when it's all fixed up, and two…I just don't think she likes me.

Is that all, he says and lifts the binoculars up from his chest and squints his eyes through them and works the dial on the bridge.

She barely says five words to me in a day.

Why is that a problem?

You don't have to work with her.

He rests the glasses back down on the log and stares over the valley.

I had a bloke work for me once, he says. Robert Sims. He was older than me but he was on my team. If you could get a good morning out of him when you got to the office you'd have done well. The lads called him Granite Bob because he was a hatchet-faced bastard who never gave you the time of day. I knew him thirty years but couldn't say where he lived, what he liked, what his wife was called or if he had any kids. I used to shudder at the thought of being alone with him for more than five minutes because he turned the air around him cold.

He died of something to do with his liver the year before he was due to retire and at his funeral I got talking to a woman from a charity who told me he had lost a daughter when she was just a child and he had given almost every penny he ever made to paediatric cancer care. Left his estate to them in his will. The man was something of a hero in what he did for those kids and he never mentioned it to me once.

The girl lifts her hands. What the fuck has that got to

do with anything?

Don't be thick, he says, picking up the glasses and forcing himself to his feet with the stick. Nancy doesn't dislike you. No more than anyone else. Let's push on before that lot blows over.

The girl looks over the valley to where scoops of heavy cloud are falling over the ridge and rolling down the slope into the acid yellow squares of rape and the darker green bands of pasture. She screws the foil into her pocket and falls in behind him as he picks his way down the slope. They descend to a narrow road on the valley floor and walk through a hamlet of biscuit coloured cottages. A brook sucks and gushes through a cobbled trench by the pavement and cuts under the road and away into the black tunnel of a laurel wood. At a junction they turn up onto the hill again and pass the carved stone arch of a manor house entrance, the gravelled driveway curving away between cliffs of immaculately cut hedge. The girl stops and peers through the ironwork gate. The gravel opens out onto a broad courtyard and a fleet of expensive vehicles and a four-storey house clad in ivy.

A man in blue overalls mulches a rose bed from a wheelbarrow and another drags a long pole through an ornamental pond. She counts twenty windows in the front façade of the house alone and wonders what anybody could do with so much space.

She turns to the road and John's receding shape and skips up the hill to catch him.

You'll be late, he says.

I know, she says, between breaths. I was just looking at the house.

Nice place.

Do you know who lives there?

He stops to look back over his shoulder in the direction of the house where only chimney pots are visible above a high brick perimeter.

No. Should I?

Just seems like a lot of house. I mean, for one family.

He starts back up the hill.

Must cost a fortune, she says.

I don't imagine it was cheap. There's a few of them around though, old manor houses. Could have been in the family for generations but I doubt it. New money most probably.

They walk on in silence until the road levels out onto a flat table of farmland and they cross through a field of green wheat under a rapidly bruising sky. At the foot of their village they meet the rain and John pulls his cap to his ears and doubles his step towards his house. She canters through the back streets and into the garden and the guesthouse and throws off her coat and quickly swaps her boots for the white pumps. With no watch or phone to know the time she prays she isn't late and will only know if Nancy is already closing down the kitchen. She bolts through the kitchen door and slows in relief to find it empty. She pads silently to the beaded curtain and can hear Nancy talking at the counter and recognises the other voice as the boy from the pub across the street who comes every day to collect a bag of pastries.

She levels her breath as she starts to load the machine from the heap of dirty crockery on the counter. Nancy appears around the corner and balances another tray on the pile.

You're late, she says flatly, and turns back through the curtain.

The girl sighs and fingers the switch on the machine. She scrapes the residues of food out from the corners of some plastic tubs into the bin and throws them into the sink and releases the tap. She scrubs down the oven top and counter and as she collects the mop and bucket from the cupboard she hears the bell sound above the café door as the boy departs. Nancy cuts through the kitchen and into the garden to smoke. The girl fills the bucket and swabs the floor, sliding it backwards towards the door and when she gets there she leans the mop handle against the architrave and steps out into the courtyard.

The rain has paused beneath gloomy bands of cloud and Nancy sits at the bench beneath the window with a trowel on her lap, looking up through the tepid colours of the garden.

She draws her head towards the girl but doesn't look up. Did you clean the tubs?

Yep.

And stack them?

Yep

And clean the filter on the machine?

I did it this morning.

Good.

The girl reaches up above the door and runs the backs of her fingers down a head of wisteria. She looks back at Nancy and sees her picking dirt off the tip of the trowel.

Think it'll rain again? Asks the girl.

Looks like it.

She stands in silence and then clears her throat and pushes herself off the door frame She shifts her weight around her feet and heads up the path to the guesthouse. She circles at the door and tells Nancy to watch the wet floor in the kitchen.

Twenty-Three

AT the bottom of the garden by the gate stands an ornamental cherry tree with boughs of sugar white blossom. The girl stands at the kitchen window and sips her tea and watches the sleeves of flower flicker in the breeze that swoops in and out of the enclosed courtyard. The sun is warm through the glass and fresh and white on the stonework and lights the thin wings of butterflies beating madly at the air beneath the window.

She has been watching the blossom mature for a fortnight, her increased efficiency in the kitchen providing ever more opportunity to stand around and think. She senses that her time there is coming to an end. The work in the guesthouse is almost complete. The appliances have been connected and the walls have taken their first coat of paint. Yesterday she overheard Nancy talking to a customer about the arrival of some new furniture. She wants to ask her directly but despite her best efforts to foster some connection, Nancy still treats her with the same detached indifference and she sees no indication that it's going to change.

She needs to make plans. She still has most of the money Suni gave her but no clearer idea of what to do with it. She stews in her naivety and the thought of how easily she was seduced by the possibility of finding something permanent and hopeful and good here in this toytown village and feels the gnarly protective instincts she honed on the streets returning. She thinks back to those bleak, unforgiving nights, huddled into cold corners with an echo in her belly and then of Suni and her invitation to join her down in London.

She places the cup on the sill and looks back through the window at the swaying cloth limbs of the cherry tree and the flakes of fallen blossom spinning on the flagstones and firms her resolve. She strides through the kitchen door and across the courtyard into the guesthouse to find her bag. From the inside pocket she pulls out the envelope and extracts the slip of paper with the scribbled number and pokes it into her bra. For more than a week she has been working the courage to ask Nancy about the telephone but is relaxed and unburdened in the relief of not having to earn the woman's affection and trust now she is reconciled to her departure.

She leans around the door to the café and finds Nancy totting figures on a pad at the counter. The café is half-full and another group of people are unzipping their coats by the door.

Hey, she says and Nancy slips her a look and then back at her pad.

Nancy, she says sharply. Can I use the telephone for a minute?

Nancy turns slowly towards her.

What telephone? She looks up and around the café. We haven't got a phone in here.

I know that, but you must have one upstairs.

She turns back to the pad. I don't want you upstairs, she says. That's my private space.

The girl laughs sarcastically. Really?

Really.

Ok then. I'm going out for a bit.

She walks back through the kitchen to the guesthouse and collects some money and is out into the garden and through the gate. She walks around the block to the main street and searches for a phone box amongst the stream of tourists. She finds one by the pub but it doesn't have a telephone inside, just a machine for starting up people's hearts.

She leans back against the box, staring into the dark window of the pub. A couple in matching yellow raincoats are hovering by the door and peering over their glasses at the menu on the wall She skirts around them and pushes through the door. Inside the air is still and smells of old carpets. The boy who collects the pastries from the café is filling a pint glass from a curved brass tap at the bar. He looks at her briefly and then handles the drinks onto the rubber mats on the bar top and takes a card from a woman and slides it into the machine. He waits for the receipt to spit out and tears it off and places it with the card back into her hands.

The girl is at the bar on her elbows and waits for him to finish.

Hi, she says. Have you got a phone in here?

A payphone?

Yeah.

Not in the bar. He says it slowly, like an explanation.

She drops her head onto her hands.

Why is this so hard, she moans.

You need a phone?

She looks up.

Obviously.

He pats around his pockets and then reaches back to shelf and hands her a device.

You can use this if you want.

She brightens. Seriously?

Yeah. He wags his fingers to take it back and thumbs in the code and hands it back over to her.

Thanks, she says. I just need to make a really quick call. I can pay you for it.

He just laughs and turns to another customer at the bar and listens for the order.

She slides into a corner and scans her eyes around the room and then reaches into her bra for the note and keys in the number. Her heart lifts in excitement at hearing Suni's voice and then cools as the tone rings out into the answering message. She taps the red circle and walks back to the bar with a grim look.

Thanks, he says, taking the phone and skimming it back onto the shelf. You alright?

Yeah, she says. She's still standing at the bar.

You want a drink?

I don't really drink.

Sounds dehydrating.

She rolls her eyes, but when she looks back up he has a

confident grin and whole brown eyes and she realises this is the first time she has ever really noticed his face. She feels some energy in the floor of her stomach that makes her want to both run and stay.

I can make you a coffee.

Nah, you're alright. I've got to get back to work.

Fair one. You work in Nancy's kitchen?

She affects a dramatic look. Not for long.

Why's that?

I don't really work there, like, for money. She just lets me stay in the guesthouse out the back for cleaning pots and mopping the floor and stuff, but it was only while she was renovating it for tourists and it's almost done, so I guess she'll be kicking me out soon enough.

She said that?

She doesn't say anything to me. It's like talking to a wall, but I know I'm not wanted.

That's a shame. Can you pull pints?

She opens up her face. Why, is there a job?

Dunno. Maybe. Summer's coming.

She pegs back her smile and then thinks about where she would stay and then she thinks about Suni again and how much she wants to see her.

Reckon I'm just gonna move on.

He shrugs pleasantly. Oh well. Let me know if you change your mind and I'll ask my Dad about a job.

Thanks, she says and looks around at the sparsely populated bar. Doesn't seem that hard.

He laughs and reaches back to the shelf for his phone. She waves goodbye and pushes the door into the street where the light is dusty and warm and people are down to their shirt sleeves and pushing sunglasses onto their heads to peer into the shop windows.

She slims herself through the crowd towards the café door, enters under the silver tinkle of the bell and sees Nancy turn from the coffee machine and lean back against it. The girl stops on the mat and they swap hostile glances. Without breaking the stare the girl walks to a table, collects some dirty plates and cups and takes them through the beads into the kitchen. Then she's back out, clearing more tables with her chin up, challenging her to say something. Nancy watches her with her thick arms folded under her chest.

The girl returns to her chores in the kitchen, rotating the crockery through the machine and cleaning out the empty tubs. Nancy stomps in and out of the kitchen throughout the lunchtime rush, their antipathy growing malignantly with every heavy drop of plates on the counter and each brooding sideways glance.

It's late in the afternoon and the girl is cleaning down the stove top when she hears the bell sound and the death of voices in the café. She slows and stops and hears Nancy lock the door and then her heavy footsteps tamping over the wooden boards. She comes through the curtain with a teapot and dark and tightened eyes.

She places the pot on the counter and drums her fingers onto the lid, watching the girl scrubbing.

What do you think you are doing?

The girl stands up from the oven and wipes back a loop of hair from her glistening forehead.

What?

I thought we already said that I didn't need you out front.

Did we?

Yes, we did. I did. You're not supposed to be out there. Just stay in here from now on. I only need you in here.

The girl shakes her head and leans back on the sponge and fingers it into the metal stove top and feels her blood bulging in her wrists and temples and blows the hair up out of her face as she scrubs.

You're going to scratch that surface if you...

Will you fucking leave it alone! She shouts and throws the scrubber against the wall. Nancy stiffens and takes a half-step back. The girl rounds on her and points a rubber yellow finger to Nancy's face.

If you don't want me here then just fucking say it! Don't keep pissing me off and ignoring me and making me out to be a be a fucking burden like I need your fucking charity or this fucking shitty job. Alright?

Calm down.

You calm down. Did I do something wrong? I fucking work as hard as I can just to get some recognition out of you and maybe try to be friends or something and you look at me like I'm the scum of the fucking earth. Tell me what I did wrong!

Nancy's hands are up in front of her and her mouth opens to speak but the girl's face is purple with invective still to come. She's reaching around her back to untie the apron.

I've known people living on the streets with nothing to their name, not a fucking bed to lie in or food to eat with warmer hearts than you, but I guess that's what it is. You know that's where I've come from and you didn't want me here from the start.

She bundles the apron and throws it into the sink as she

makes for the door.

I'll get my shit and go. It'll save you the fucking awkwardness of having to ask me to leave.

She storms out through the garden and into the guesthouse and throws the door behind her.

Twenty-Four

SHE'S on the sofa in the dark with her knees up to her chin. Her bag is against the wall, packed and ready to go with the sleeping sack rolled and tied beneath it. She winds the bracelet slowly round her finger and then pulls it taut and winds it again as she reviews her options. Her pride wants her out, now, but the only realistic option tonight is John's shed and to return to it means the kind of defeat her pride also wants to avoid.

She yawns and stretches out her legs. She'll sleep on the sofa and then leave before Nancy wakes in the morning. She'll go and see Suni and if she has already left for London she'll get herself a hotel and try to find some work. She steels herself to the thought but can't deny the inner truth. The idea of going back there makes her feel sick. Maybe she'll go somewhere else.

Through the window she sees the light open up in the courtyard and then a tap at the door.

Shit, she says, and wishes she'd made for the shed.

She clears her throat and says, It's open.

The door swings open and Nancy is there in jeans and a white jumper with blue hoops, half her face in shade, the other shining in gold from the courtyard light. Her hair is wet and down by her ears. The girl has never seen her with her hair down.

Come on, she says and walks back into the light towards the kitchen.

The girl holds her scathing frown and waits. Then she sighs and pushes off from the sofa and slips the bracelet into her pocket and walks grudgingly through the courtyard and into the kitchen. The door to the stairs of Nancy's flat is open. She peeks into the glum depths of the café and then around the door and up the stairs and ascends them slowly. The stairs open into a lounge poorly lit by standing lamps and there's a sofa and matching armchair screening a television set and a circular dining table with some hard chairs beneath the window.

Nancy comes from another door with a bottle lodged under her arms and a pair of tumblers pinched in her fingers.

Have a seat, she says, indicating the table beneath the window by settling the bottle there.

The girl walks to the table and pulls out the chair and sits with her hands on her lap. Nancy lights a cigarette, pulls out the cork from the bottle and twists a finger of brown liquid into the glasses.

Have a drink.

The girl gives a little laugh through her nose. Everyone is trying to get me drunk today, she says.

How's that?

Nothing. It was just the guy in the pub.

Nancy collects an ashtray from the floor by the sofa.

He's a nice boy.

He's alright.

Do you not drink?

The girl rolls the glass in her hand. What is it?

Brandy.

She sniffs at it and pulls up her head. Not really.

Hang on then. Nancy goes back into the kitchen and returns with a large bottle of coke. She fizzes off the cap and sloshes some into the glass. The girl lets it froth and simmer and takes a sip.

That's alright.

Nancy grunts and holds the bottle up to scan the label. If I could afford the good stuff I wouldn't want to see it diluted, but it hardly matters with this. She sits and slides her cigarette into a cut niche in the glass ashtray and takes a sip of her drink and sucks at her lips.

They sit for a few seconds and the mantelpiece clock clicks crisply. Then Nancy draws herself onto her elbows.

I want you to know you can use the telephone.

Thanks.

I also want...I also want you to know. She stops. That you don't have to leave.

The girl recognises she occupies the higher ground, but isn't inclined to exploit it.

I don't want to leave.

Good.

But I don't want to feel like I'm not welcome, or that I'm not doing a good enough job. I'm sorry for kicking off and that, but I can't work you out. It's like you'd already decided that I wasn't to be trusted and you'd only let me be here as a favour to John and you were just waiting until the guesthouse was finished so you could move me on and to be fair I've worked really hard and...

Nancy waves her hand up from her glass and is nodding her head with the start of a smile and the girl thinks that it's the first time she has seen her smile and that despite some unwanted weight on her she has an attractive and noble face. Nancy slides her fingers over her temple and down behind her ear and turns in the chair to cross her legs.

Let's just be really honest with each other and then we know where we stand, she says, picking up the cigarette and tapping off the ash into the tray.

Ok.

Yes, I took you on as a favour to John, but not out of charity. You can see how much I need the help. I wasn't thrilled about the fact that you'd come in off the streets, but I'm suspicious enough about things at the best of times and you were dirty and ragged and had a bit of an attitude. I just presumed you were going to hang around for a few days and then go. Or trash the place.

The girl swigs her drink and feels the warmth bloom in her chest and slip through her arms and legs.

Yeah, well. I didn't. I've been here a month and it's like living through a Siberian winter with you.

Nancy fidgets in the chair and refills the tumblers. The girl tops hers up with more coke.

I've got my own issues. That's not your fault.

The girl feels a tug at the base of her throat.

Look, if I don't have to go then that's alright with me. I can do more to help you out. I can serve in the café and help in the garden. I see you in there in the evening. You mope around there without really doing anything like you don't know what else to do with yourself. I'm sitting in there bored as fuck, but don't want to ask if I can do anything.

Nancy is staring into her glass, her chest heaving slowly.

I'm sorry, says the girl. I'm not trying to be out of order.

Nancy looks up keenly at the girl.

You're a tough kid.

Yeah, right.

I mean it. I know what it's like to have it hard.

The girl blinks and starts to speak but when she blinks again her eyes are stinging.

You want to tell me about it? Nancy asks.

Not really.

Nancy lays her hand over the girls and leaves it there a while.

The girl draws her sleeve across her eyes.

What about you? She says.

Nancy fills herself another drink and collects a pocket of breath and lets it go.

She says she doesn't trust people any more. She says she had a husband who liked to drink because he thought he'd failed in life but didn't have the courage to do anything about it. So he'd drink and then he'd come after her and direct his hatred and his inadequacy against the only person who cared enough to help him because her compassion only revealed in him the depths of his weakness. He wasn't a bad man at heart but he exhausted all her ultimatums so she divorced him and took a parcel of cash and tried to build a little business in the clean air of a tourist village away from where he could bother her. When he finally tracked her down, he smashed the place into kindling and was carted off by the police.

That morning when they took him away, she says, staring reflectively into the empty tumbler, I was sitting in the wreckage wondering how I was going ever going to make it right. I looked up and saw John standing at the door asking if I was still serving.

The girl smiles.

Nancy drills her fag into the glass ashtray, lights another and looks out through the window to the blackness beyond the village lights. The girl studies her as she smokes.

Has he ever been back?

Nancy tightens her eyes. No. But the thought that he might never leaves you.

The girl gulps at her drink. Sounds like a wanker.

She laughs smoke through her teeth and then settles and watches over the girl.

You have some family? She asks.

The girl shrugs.

What about that tattoo?

She revolves her wrist to show the mark and rubs her thumb along it.

First love?

You could say that.

Nothing to be ashamed of. I've got one on my hip that I wish I could...

It was for my Dad.

Oh.

The girl pulls up a painful look.

Nancy pours them both another drink. You don't have to talk about it love.

The girl rolls her head. What, after you gave me the

whole story of your life.

It's not a competition.

I didn't mean it like that.

It's ok. I'm not prying.

She fingers the rim of her glass and then drinks and swallows it hard. The clock beats out the empty seconds while Nancy sits and smokes.

He had leukaemia. He died.

I'm sorry.

Yeah.

When was that?

Three years ago.

That's not fair. No-one should have to deal with that.

The girl wipes her nose with the back of her hand as she lifts the tumbler to her mouth.

No, she says, but we did.

And your Mum?

She shoots her a straight look and Nancy can see she is straddling the boundary between going any further and locking back up, but the drink is pulling her forward.

Mum was amazing, she says. To start with. She just made it alright, for me and my brother, like it was almost something that made us special. Just the three of us, you know. But I guess she got bored of that.

What makes you say that?

The girls shrugs and grabs the bottle and slops some into her glass and leans the bottle across the table towards Nancy's tumbler and some of it bounces out of the glass onto the table.

Nancy wipes her hand across it and rubs her thumb and forefinger together. She found another man, she says.

Yeah, says the girl, slurring now. She found another man.

And?

He was alright.

But he wasn't your dad.

Nope. But look, he's a man. What's he gonna do, not try and make the rules? Fuck his rules.

Nancy lights another cigarette and sits staring. The girl drains her drink and humps herself to the sofa, hugs a pillow to her chest and tries to quell the spinning.

Twenty-Five

WHEN she wakes the sun is spread across the table beneath the window and twisting through the empty bottle and the rim of the ashtray into astral squares of colour on the walls and dust is hazing through the blade of light like smoke. She pushes the blanket down her body and swings her legs around and pushes her finger tips into the soreness in her neck. Her mouth is dry and sticky and she needs to piss.

She stares through her feet to the tide of voices in the café below. She wonders of the time and knows it must be late for the sun to be over the garden wall and for the café to be so full and thinks she might be in for some trouble but then rewinds through the night with Nancy at the table and knows the landscape has changed.

As she stands her head is heavy and her stomach feels active and watery. She slumps into the bathroom and sits on the bowl. She finishes and wipes herself and then swabs her face before taking down four handfuls of water. On her way back through the sitting room she sees the phone on the wall and stops. She fingers around her bra and is surprised to find the scrap of paper still there. She lifts up the receiver and thumbs in the numbers and pushes it up to her face and waits as it runs through to the automated message.

She looks around the airless room and drops her feet down the stairs, her head jarring with every step. She goes to the kitchen and fills a glass of water and drinks it at the window, watching the fallen puffs of cherry blossom skitter around the courtyard.

She hears Nancy rattle some plates onto the counter and turns with a wounded look she hopes will serve as an apology.

Hey.

Nancy is relaxed and smiling. How did you sleep?

I'm a bit stiff. Sorry I'm late. I'm not used to drinking.

Don't worry. It's not even busy. Get in and have a shower and get changed. I'll sort us through lunch and then when it's quieter I'll show you how to work the coffee machine and the till.

You gonna let me out front?

Might as well get you doing some proper work.

The girl leans back on the sink and drinks her water and lets herself enjoy it. Then she swills out the glass and walks out through the courtyard and into the guesthouse. Her bag is still packed by the door. She carries it into the bedroom and transfers the clothes onto the bed and the bag of toiletries to the bathroom. She takes a long shower and dresses and paints some colour around her eyes.

Back in the café there are people waiting to be served so she takes a pad from the counter and without any instruction from Nancy, takes an order and rips it off the pad and hands it to her as she passes back through the beaded curtain to the kitchen to prepare the food.

Through the afternoon they work together like the sliding parts of the same machine, cohesive and compact and despite the cobwebs of drink the girl is quick to learn and finds a heady pleasure in being released from the boredom of the kitchen into the life and laughs of the café.

Nancy is showing her how to work the till when the boy from the pub comes in to ask about pastries. They both look to an empty display and then to each other. Nancy excuses herself into the kitchen. The boy is at the counter, taut with muscle beneath his thin shirt and bold chords of tendon roped into his neck.

Pastries are all gone, says the girl. Don't you normally come in the morning?

Yeah, he says. But we had a delivery. So…

So…we're all out, she says.

Alright, he says and shrugs and looks at the case.

She perks at a thought. Have you still got that phone?

Yeah, he says and slides his hand into his jeans.

Do you mind?

No, help yourself.

Thanks. Sit over there and I'll make you a tea.

Can you do me a coffee?

She looks at him narrowly.

Tea's alright, he says.

She goes into the kitchen and clicks on the kettle. Then she slips back through the courtyard into the guesthouse to find the number.

She walks back with the phone to her ear, thinking of the boy and waiting for the tone to run to the answering service, resolving to leave a message this time.

Hello.

She stops under the wisteria by the kitchen door and turns back to face the sunshine pouring over the garden wall.

Hey. Suni?

Who is this?

It's me. How are you doing? I've been trying to call.

Who?

Fuck's sake Suni, It's me.

A pause and then Suni's voice is low and toneless. Hey babe, she says. I didn't know you had a phone.

I don't. It's not mine. It doesn't matter. How are you?

I'm ok. How are you?

The girl's energy is flattened. I'm doing really good. Got a job and everything.

That's really good babe. Where are you?

Up in the countryside. Where are you?

I'm still here.

In the city?

Yeah.

How come?

We've just not managed to sort it out yet.

Shit Sun, I'm sorry. How is it?

A longer pause. It's not getting any better.

Is it really bad?

It is what it is. It wasn't ever fun.

I really thought you would have left by now. In my head you and Cam were already in that dress shop.

Not yet.

When do you think it's going to happen?

I dunno.

Can I help?

It's ok, she says. We're big girls. But you sound great babe, you sound really...happy.

It's ok up here, she says. Had to sleep in a shed for a bit, but there are some nice people around.

That makes me happy, I'm glad you called. I'm glad you're ok, but look babe, I've got to go but I'll speak to you soon yeah?

Sure, says the girl as the line drops. She holds the phone on her chest and walks back into the café where the boy is playing with a flower stalk from one of the ribbed vases at a table.

He smiles. I forgot to say. My dad says we're gonna need someone soon if you still need a job. He just needs to have a bit of chat.

Really?

Yeah.

Just tell me when to come over.

Tomorrow?

Ok.

She pushes herself up and starts to smarten up the chairs around the tables and collects some cups and takes them into the kitchen and fills the machine. She wipes down the counter and brings out the brush to sweep the floor as the boy plays with his phone and slowly drinks his tea. When she brings out the mop he stands awkwardly and reminds her to come over tomorrow.

I will, she says.

As she locks the door behind him Nancy appears through the beads with a spool of paper and an amused grin. The girl slops the mop head into the pail and pretends not to notice.

Leave that for a bit and let me show you how to change the roll.

The girl leans the handle against the back of a chair and goes up to the counter where Nancy is lifting up the plastic hood from the till.

You have to free these clips and then slide it onto this tube.

Ok.

Then wind it back under here and clip it back in.

Does it matter which way it goes round?

Yes. Always from the bottom.

Let me try.

Nancy shuffles over.

He likes you.

I know he does.

Why are you blushing then?

I'm just concentrating.

Of course you are. Feed it from the bottom.

I can do it. She winds the roll around on the spool and fingers back the clips and replaces the hood. Nancy taps at some buttons and the thing bites onto the paper and spits an edge up through the slot. Nancy tears it off and tucks it into her apron pocket.

Not interested?

He's alright.

Nancy whistles through her teeth. If I was twenty years younger you wouldn't have a chance. Nice arms.

Alright perv.

She crackles a laugh. You look shattered. Why don't you turn in. I'll finish up in the kitchen.

The girl yawns and looks up through the big window

into the street where the evening sun coats the road with a mellow brassy light and makes a shadow of the last few tourists stopping with their hands cupped around their faces to peer through the glass.

I think I will, she says.

Twenty-Six

SHE stops and rests her hand upon the damp wood of the gate and can see him through the milky light, hacking the spade into the soil. She pushes into the allotment and walks the dewy grass path between the brown beds of earth.

He sees her coming and leans on the spade with a suspicious smile.

You're up early. I know you've not come to help.

I couldn't sleep, she says.

Guilty conscience, he says still, smiling and lifting up a shard of shining black earth and turning it back onto the ground and breaking it down with the back of his spade. Despite the morning chill there are runs of sweat on his neck.

What do you mean?

It's just an old saying. If people can't sleep.

Oh.

Why don't you pour us some tea. He points at the shed. You know where everything is.

She nods and walks into the gloom of the shed and

smells the air and smiles fondly at the memory of sleeping there. She recognises it as a junction of her life, where unpleasant memories terminate and better ones begin and as she collects the cups she can hear John humming and realises that it wasn't the shed that was the junction.

He's down to his shirt sleeves when she comes back out with the tea and another row of earth is rolled before him.

He takes the cup and looks around a colourless sky slung low over the houses of the village. She sits on the bench and blows at the tea.

Some fog this morning, he says. Reckon the sun will burn through it by this afternoon.

She mumbles some agreement.

How's it going with Nancy?

Despite her mood she permits a happy grin. Getting better, she says. We had a big dust-up but then she was really cool with me and now it's all good.

Told you. Some things just need a bit of time.

Don't you ever get tired of being right?

He laughs and places the cup into the grass and slides up the spade and heels it back into the ground.

I got another job too.

Did you? Where's that then?

At the pub.

Which one.

The Lion.

Nice pub.

I've only done a few nights but it's ok.

Good for you.

She sits and watches him work the soil. In the trees to her right above the hedgerow, heavy black birds survey the misty fields and croak dryly. John finishes another row and stands and waves at someone coming in through the gate at the far side of the allotment. He turns on the girl sitting and staring into her tea and whistles.

Get into that shed and fetch me a rake will you. And when you come out tell me what's up. You've a face as dark as a miner's thumb.

She stands and gets the rake and hands it over to him. He takes the shaft and uses the end to clear some clots of mud from his boots. She drops back onto the bench and he starts to pull the soil back and forth with the rake, waiting for her to talk.

I could do with a bit of advice though, she says eventually.

No shame in it. What's up?

She scratches a nail into the arm of the bench. It's been bothering me all week. Before that actually, but more since I spoke to her.

Who?

A friend from when I lived in the city. Then she laughs. If you can call sleeping in alleyways living somewhere.

What's up with your friend?

She winces a little and watches the care with which he tends the soil, gently levelling it back and forth.

She's a prostitute.

Oh, he says. Does that matter?

Not to me.

Is she in trouble?

I think so.

What sort of trouble has she got?

The girl searches for the right words to use. John lays down the rake and walks behind the shed and comes back with a tray of small plants and kneels to the prepared soil and starts to prise them from their pots. The girl is still on the bench, wrestling with her thoughts.

Tell me if you think it will help, he says. You or her. If not, just let it sit. If I'm ever in two minds, I try to ignore them both.

A sudden smack of noise reports from over the fields and the birds scatter from their perches and winch themselves over the trees. She watches them flee and considers the advice.

He can feel her silence on his back.

You've not been out walking he says, thumbing a plant into the soil.

I know, she says. I've been working though.

Where are we today? He says, scooping a hole from the soil to insert another plug. Friday today. I've got to take the wife to the doctors tomorrow but I'll be out Sunday morning if you're interested.

Alright, she says. I don't work Sunday mornings. Come round about nine.

He holds a plant up to his eyes and pinches out some browning leaves. The day is half gone by then. I'll be at the gate just after seven.

Twenty-Seven

SHE slides from beneath the covers and treads silently through the lounge in her shorts and vest and quietly unlocks the door. The courtyard is still and the cool air lifts the hair on her bare arms. She slips back into the guesthouse and pulls a blanket from the back of the sofa and throws it around her shoulders and pads back out.

Above her the sky is a creamy blue canvas and promises a day of unbroken sunshine and supple warm breezes, where the spring finally turns to summer and all bitter traces of winter have been burnt away. She walks up the path along the flower beds, frothing with forget-me-not and the tall nodding bonnets of aquilegia, all cast in a slate blue shadow. At the cherry tree by the gate, tiny birds shake from the branches and glide up onto the garden wall and chitter irritably at the disturbance.

She opens the garden gate and looks up the street to the east and an eager young sun building over the hills. A sleek ginger cat watches her from a wall, its auburn fur aflame in the light. The girl closes her eyes and rests her face in the sun.

Back in the courtyard she looks to Nancy's flat but the blinds are still down. She makes herself a tea and takes it back out to the bench. She hinges her knees up to her chin and drinks the tea and watches the courtyard brighten and the hoverflies sawing around the flowers and feels drowsy and calm. She pours the dregs into a flower pot and slouches back inside.

In the half-light of her bedroom the boy's exposed back shines whitely on the bed beneath the window. She sits on the edge of the bed and leans over him to smell his skin and then pulls the cover up over his shoulder. He moans and rolls his head to face her but his eyes don't open and his hair flops over his face.

She collects some clothes from the pile in the corner and takes them into the lounge and pulls them on. She ties up her pumps and tears a chunk of bread from a loaf by the sink and daubs it with chocolate spread and closes the door quietly behind her.

John is resting against the wall opposite the gate under the watchful eyes of the cat.

Ready?

Ready.

We're in no rush, he says tapping his stick into the cobbles and lifting it to the bread in her hand. You could have finished your breakfast.

It's ok.

Who eats chocolate for breakfast?

I do. Where are we headed?

We'll go down the valley and then up through the wood behind Aston and come back round.

Ok.

They walk through the broad blanket of sunlight and then cut from the alley into the main village road and follow it until they get to the church. They stop in the graveyard under the shade of a broad yew and John peels off his jumper and ties it around his waist and looks up around the sky and says it's going to be a scorcher.

You can feel it, she says. It's one of those mornings where you just know.

They follow the cemetery wall out through a gate and then across another road into a field sloping gently down towards the valley. On the valley floor a hamlet slumbers in shadow and a light shroud of mist, waiting for the sun to crest the slopes and burn away the moisture. John takes the gradient cautiously, leaning on his stick and prodding it into the ground below him to test it for his feet. The girl follows, dodging the cowpats in her white pumps and collecting yellow stalks of rattle into a pocket bouquet. When she has enough flowers she finds a tough cord of grass and ties it together.

The hamlet is Sunday silent. A woman washes her windows and another plants bulbs in a border. Through an open door a radio talks in a hushed voice. The air is much cooler now and John shivers as they pass along the sandstone houses and converted barns. At a pond she wants to stop and watch the ducks but he complains that he's cold and wants to get moving back up the hill.

There's a farm at the top, he says. We can have a minute up there.

They cross a wooden bridge and take a track up through crumbling, mossy-rocked walls into a birch wood until the sunlight gilds the leaves in shimmering slips of green and gold and falls in pockets of light through the branches to the floor. John begins to blow and she slows her pace to keep him with her and when the path levels off and the canopy thins above them the heat sits on their backs and he points his stick at the farm.

They stop at an old grindstone in a circular trough by the farmhouse gate and John leans his stick against the lip and wipes his forehead with a blue handkerchief he produces from his sleeve.

The girl sits on the lip and touches the flowerheads bedded into the trough and looks out across the flat fields, wavering in a gentle haze of heat. He sits next to her and tucks the cloth back into his cuff.

How come we never came up this way before? She asks.

He shrugs. We're lucky. You can walk every day of the year and not do the same route twice. They're foaling in that field. I thought you might want to see them.

She smiles and twists the yellow bouquet on her lap. I've always loved horses. Since I was a kid. My dad always promised me a pony but what dad doesn't.

He grunts.

There's something about them that you can't work out. A contradiction. They're noble and free but there's a sadness in their eyes cos they know that they're still slaves to something.

Like people, he says.

She looks up over the fields to a fleet of sculpted white clouds running across the swathe of blue sky and exhales slowly.

Maybe, she says. Let's go have a look.

They stand and walk the rutted track to a break in the hedge and lean through it into the field. A knock-kneed foal prances around a chestnut mare and nuzzles its head up under her to feed. She bunts it away with her hips and clips the grass with her teeth. The foal stands off and watches her and then makes another pass.

They continue along the track under the heaving sun and the pasture gives way to ripening wheat on either side, rippling in a thin breeze and the dark shadows of the clouds pass through it like ships. They cut across a busy road and then onto a heath that slopes back down to the village, the girl walking in silence while John hums an ageless melody. The last of the cloud is slipping beyond the rim of the hills as they come upon the houses by the allotment wall and the heat pounding off the bricks.

John walks her back through the alley and stops at the gate. He leans to the floor and twists off a brown head of poppy, tips the seeds into his hand and scatters them back into the broken cobbles at the foot of the wall.

Say hi to Nance, he says.

The girl smiles. I will.

If you still need to talk, you know where to find me.

I do.

She lifts the latch and walks down the garden and into the guesthouse. Inside, it's cool and dark and her heart rings at the thought that the boy might still be there in her bed. He isn't, but a note sits waiting for her on the pillow.

She reads it and laughs and folds it into a square and puts it into the inside pocket of her bag with the bracelet. She takes a quick shower and dresses for work.

Nancy is in the kitchen frying bacon. She sees the girl

come through the door beneath the wisteria and fails to hide a knowing look.

Good night?

The girl shakes her head as she ties the apron around her waist.

Not bad. You?

She just laughs and turns the meat in the pan.

Finish this one, will you love, she says and hands her the spatula. It's two egg and bacon on brown.

The girl nods and takes the wooden spatula, lays it on the counter and clicks on the kettle. Nancy disappears through the beads.

She works through the afternoon with a diverted mind. It pulls her back to her conversation with Suni and her inability to make contact with her since but then onwards to the boy and the idea of him again. She supplies sandwiches into the glass display and loads the dishwasher with dirty plates and scribbles orders onto her pad. When the pace drops off Nancy takes the chance to instruct her on the coffee machine and its peculiar ways. She burns a couple of roasts and exhausted by the walk and her lack of sleep, asks if she can pick it up tomorrow.

That's fine, says Nancy, still holding the same satirical grin. Just clear down the tables and call it a day.

She tucks her pad into the front pouch of her apron and swirls around the counter. She collects the plates from two of the tables into a pile and balances some cups on top. She centres a flower vase, collects a discarded newspaper under her arm and takes the tower of crockery into the kitchen.

The machine is still humming on the end of its cycle. She lowers the plates onto the counter and turns to rest on the edge of the sink. She takes the paper and folds it out in front of her, narrowing her tired eyes to read.

The headline talks of death in the lanes. She stiffens on the lip of the sink and reads of the discovery of two female bodies in the woods near Naunton, somewhere between the ages of twenty five and thirty. Her fists tighten around the edges of the paper and she fast scans the type to find a name or physical description and then flicks quickly through the pages to find the rest of the story. She reads it all and then reads it again, her heart drumming in her belly.

She lays the paper on the counter as the machine on the wall announces the end of its cycle with a ping.

She feels the sweat run coldly on her back as she steps out through the kitchen and into the soft warm light of the courtyard. She lowers herself onto the bench beneath the window and looks down the garden to where the last of the white cherry blossom has fallen.

Acknowledgements

A great many thanks to the editorial and design teams at époque press for all their work in bringing this book to life and to Laura, just for listening.